ALSO BY ARANKA SIEGAL

Upon the Head of the Goat
A Childhood in Hungary 1939–1944

Grace in the Wilderness
After the Liberation 1945–1948

MEMORIES *of* BABI

MEMORIES *of* BABI

Stories by
Aranka Siegal

FARRAR ❧ STRAUS ❧ GIROUX

NEW YORK

Distributed in Canada by Douglas & McIntyre Ltd.
Printed in the United States of America
Designed by Robbin Gourley
First edition, 2008
1   3   5   7   9   10   8   6   4   2

www.fsgkidsbooks.com

Library of Congress Cataloging-in-Publication Data
Siegal, Aranka.
    Memories of Babi / Aranka Siegal.— 1st ed.
        p.   cm.
    ISBN-13: 978-0-374-39978-8
    ISBN-10: 0-374-39978-6
    1. Siegal, Aranka—Juvenile literature.   2. Siegal, Aranka—Childhood
and youth—Anecdotes—Juvenile literature.   3. Jewish children—
Hungary—Biography—Juvenile literature.   4. Grandparent and
child—Hungary—Anecdotes—Juvenile literature.   I. Title.

DS135.H93S5967 2008
947.7'9—dc22
[B]
                                                                            2007007002

*For my beloved husband, Gilbert, who always
encouraged me to write; my dedicated children, Rise
and Joseph, who are a constant source of help;
and my beautiful sister Iboya, with whom I
still reminisce about our childhood*
—A.S.

CONTENTS

MEMORIES *of* BABI

Introduction

I was born and raised in Hungary in a small city called Beregszász, but some of the most vivid memories of my childhood are of my grandmother, Babi, on her farm. She lived in the village of Komjaty, just across the Hungarian border, in the Carpathian Mountains in Ukraine. From the time I was five, my mother often sent me to visit my grandparents, and then just Babi after Grandpa died—usually during the summer, but sometimes during the other seasons as well. As a result of these visits, I could speak Hungarian, Ukrainian, and Yiddish, just like Babi, but she only wanted me to speak to her in Yiddish.

Komjaty was divided by a steep hill. On one side was Little Komjaty, which was made up of flat farmland. Most of the farmers were Christians, with just a few Jews, including Babi, among them. As far as I can remember, there was only one school in Little Komjaty, with children of different ages all in one classroom. Helping with farmwork was considered more important than going to school. Almost all Jews and Christians were very poor. Their contact was usually over work, a sick child or animal, or trading produce. There was a distinct distrust between them, yet I remember Babi was friendly with some of her Christian neighbors, perhaps because she had lived near them her whole life.

Big Komjaty was more populated, more literate; the people who lived there had bigger houses and seemed more sophisticated to me. There were stores where you could buy more than just the kerosene, candles, sugar, and salt found in Little Komjaty. There was also a larger Jewish population, but there, too, you could feel the undercurrent of anti-Semitism and separation, though it wasn't as apparent as in Little Komjaty. This was in the 1930s, just before World War II came to Hungary and Ukraine.

Even after Grandpa died, Babi never felt alone because she had such a strong belief in her God. She felt him everywhere and believed he watched over her wherever she was. Babi often quoted from her prayer books, in which the rabbis taught that all men are equal in the eyes of God, whether Jews or gentiles, rich or poor.

Babi's yard was enclosed by a low picket fence. Her whitewashed house was built out of wood and mortar and had a straw-thatched roof and dirt floors. It had two bedrooms that were separated by a kitchen in the middle of the house. The largest of the two bedrooms served as the master bedroom, dining room for the Sabbath and holiday meals, and living room. This main room had two windows, one in the front facing the road, and another in the back looking out at her fruit trees and barn. There was also a door in this room that led to a long narrow pantry. The other bedroom faced the forest and was used for guests in the spring, summer, and fall, and for storage in the winter because the only heat came from the kitchen's wood-burning stove and a hearth in the large bedroom.

The front porch was used as an "everything" room for the spring, summer, and fall. During the three seasons of good weather we ate most of our meals out there at a long wooden table. One wall of the porch and part of the straw-thatched roof were covered by grapevines that served as a living canopy. This little arbor kept us cool in the summer and provided enough grapes to eat freshly picked, make jam out of, and dry for raisins. We also used the porch to receive visitors and prepare food, and we liked to spend our leisure time there.

Babi's fields stretched from the back of her house to a river called the Rika. She grew corn, wheat, rye, sunflowers, pumpkins, and turnips. She hired families from the village to help her, and all the work on her farm was performed with hand tools and the occasional oxen-drawn plow. Babi went to bed early and rose early, her days revolving around the seasons and the sun and her work on the farm.

Babi's hands were never idle. After we washed the supper dishes, she would take off her apron, light the kerosene lamp over the table in the main room, and pick up her mending, crocheting, embroidery, or patchwork. As she taught me how to do all of these things, she would tell me stories or offer advice. Even now, I still hear her voice in my mind, and it becomes clearer and stronger, and her advice more meaningful, with every passing year.

By the time I was seven she had taught me to crochet chains, and I made my first pot holder at age eight. By age nine I had learned to darn my own stockings. Babi would guide me through each step as I held the mushroom-shaped wooden darning spool inside the stocking in my left hand and the thick needle threaded with mending yarn in my right. She would direct me to stitch close, even lines to cover the hole, and then, weaving the darning needle in and out of the lines, stitch across, back and forth, till the hole was filled in with tiny squares. By ten I had mastered embroidering napkins with the colorful cross-stitching that was characteristic of Hungarian and Czech embroidery.

"Women have to know how to do all these things, besides cooking, raising children, and cleaning house," Babi said.

I remember my family's anticipation of one of Babi's rare visits to our house in the city. Mother gathered all seven of us children in the kitchen the day before her arrival and said, "While my mother is here you must be on your best behavior. I don't want to hear any arguments—not one disagreement! You will give your grandmother the utmost respect, be polite to one another, and do everything I ask."

When we picked Babi up from the train she was wearing a brown traveling suit and a brown silk scarf over her head that was tied under her chin so only her face was uncovered. I liked it much better when she switched her scarf for a cotton kerchief, put on a light summer dress, and tied an apron around her waist—then she looked like the Babi I knew and loved. She joined Mother in the kitchen to help prepare the Sabbath dinner. I could only understand part of what they were saying because they spoke Yiddish so quickly, but I clearly understood that Mother's role had changed to that of the daughter and Babi was now the mother.

On Saturday morning Babi tried to read from her prayer book, but a constant stream of relatives and friends stopped by to visit. On Sunday she got up early, packed her satchel, and was ready to leave by the time the rest of us woke up.

I overheard my mother pleading, "Mama, you promised that this time you would stay at least a few days. What went wrong?"

"Nothing went wrong. Your children are well behaved, your household is well managed, everyone made me feel welcome. But I want to return to the farm to take care of my animals; I can't sit idly."

Mother put her hands on her hips. "So your animals need you more than I do?"

"Rise, your feelings are getting hurt and you're making me feel bad, but I worry when I leave my responsibilities in strange hands."

Babi's visit had lasted forty-eight hours.

I often find myself talking to Babi in my mind, asking her for advice and seeking her approval. I want to share my life with her, to show her all the modern changes that would make her work easier today—knowing full well that she would not like using these new devices. She would be more comfortable churning butter by hand, baking bread in a mortar oven, and working by the flickering light of a kerosene lamp—all things we would never think of doing today.

Meaningful childhood memories can last a lifetime— here are stories inspired by some of my visits with Babi.

The Feathered Spirit

I woke early one Friday morning, put on one of my cotton country dresses, and walked into the kitchen to find Babi well into her baking for the Sabbath. Her apron tied around her, her sleeves rolled up, and the babushka on her head knotted under her chin, she was standing in front of her kneading board. Her whole body swayed in rhythm as she shook the flour sifter from side to side.

"Good morning, Babi," I said.

"I'm glad you are up, Piri," said Babi, glancing quickly in my direction. "Go, *shaefele*, little lamb, and wash the sleep out of your eyes. I'll roll out a piece of challah dough, and bake you a nice *lángos*."

After I came back from the well where I had washed my face, I watched Babi's small dark fingers tear off a piece of the spongy white dough, form it into a ball, pound it with her knuckles until it was the shape of a saucer, and finally roll it flat to the size of a dinner plate. Then, lifting the stretched dough over both her hands, she carefully placed it on the long-handled bread paddle and shook it onto the hot oven floor.

Babi stopped briefly and said, "Go and pour yourself coffee; my hands are covered with flour," before she turned back to the rest of the dough. She had a system for making challah that was second nature to her hands. They seemed to move of their own accord from one step to the next until all the dough was kneaded, rolled, and braided into challah and distributed on various baking pans, which were then placed inside the hot walls of the oven.

I mixed the acorn coffee half-and-half with boiled milk, and measured out several spoonfuls of sugar. When I was done, the *lángos* was ready. It was hot and crusty and filled with holes as I pulled it apart to butter it. Babi, watching in amusement at the way I was so totally engrossed in eating my breakfast, asked if she should make me another *lángos* for when I came back.

"Where am I going?"

"I think you are now old enough to run an important errand for me. I have the chicken in a basket on the porch ready for the slaughterer. You are going to take the chicken to Big Komjaty to the *shochet*."

The hot buttery *lángos* suddenly ceased to interest me.

"Alone?"

"Sure, alone."

"I have never gone by myself before."

"Don't you know the way?"

"Yes, but . . . I'll have to walk past the cemetery . . ."

"And . . . ?"

Although I wanted to plead, "Don't send me," I knew it was no use. The cemetery and the slaughterer's were the two places I dreaded most in all Komjaty, but if Babi asked me to run an errand, I would just have to go, regardless of my fears.

"Nothing," I said in answer to Babi's question.

"Good girl. Now, don't linger or visit. Come straight back. The day goes so fast, and I will need plenty of time to prepare the chicken for the Sabbath." She went on talking, but I did not hear her words. My thoughts were on the cemetery and Noochum, the evil spirit in rooster form who haunted it.

Babi walked me out to the porch. Still talking, she hung the basket with the cackling chicken over my arm. "Go, *shaefele*. Hurry."

It was one of those days in July when the air was hot and sticky and the fields were still. Nothing stirred outside, but in me all the ghost stories I had ever heard were unfolding and leaping over each other. There were as many ghost stories in Komjaty as there were people.

The one that had made the biggest impression on me was about the Jewish cemetery and had been told to me in the courtyard of the synagogue. It was during one of the High Holy Days, when all the grownups were inside praying. The three daughters of the widow Laiku were sitting outside on the porch railing of their two-room house, which was a few meters from the synagogue. Their legs dangled over the outside of the railing. The girls were dressed in their Sabbath best and wore dark ribbed cotton stockings and high laced oxford shoes with many visible patches. For the benefit of the out-of-town children like me who were spending the holidays with relatives, they were telling stories about Komjaty.

It was Tesy, the oldest, who told the story about Noochum and the Jewish cemetery on top of the steep hill that divided Big Komjaty from Little Komjaty. She said that there had been a loyal old caretaker named Noochum who had tended the graves in the cemetery until he died at the age of ninety-three. But he could not rest in peace because he worried about the dead not being cared for. So he had come back from his grave disguised as a rooster and continued his job of caretaking. Since Noochum's grave had been dug out and found empty, there could be no doubt about the truth of the story, as all three of the widow's daughters assured us by swearing. First they spat away from themselves—"Ptui, ptui, ptui." Then Tesy jumped up and hopped around on one leg with the other tucked under her skirt and said, "I should walk like this for the rest of my life if it's not true that his grave was found empty." The middle sister got up, spat again, and declared, "I should grow boils under both arms if Tesy is not telling you the truth." Then the youngest sister stood up and covered her left eye with her left hand. "I should go blind in this eye if the story you are listening to is not exactly the way it happened."

"That is why the cemetery could never hire a new caretaker; nobody would take the job with Noochum running around all the time," Tesy concluded. "That is why the grounds look so neglected."

"Why doesn't Noochum take better care of it?" asked one of the out-of-town children.

"He is not interested in the grounds—just the dead," offered the middle sister. "Besides, did you ever see a rooster prune hedges?" Nobody had further comment after that, and ever since then I had gone to great lengths to avoid any close contact with the cemetery.

The heat of the day, coupled with my inner anxieties and the restless chicken trying to break loose from the basket, added to my burden. I decided to sit down on the side of the dusty road at the bottom of the hill from the cemetery and try to think of a way to deal with the situation. I stroked the smooth feathers of the chicken and talked to it about being good and brave. When we were both calmed down, I continued on my way.

With my head bent over the basket, I kept the conversation flowing as I walked up the hill and began to pass the length of the cemetery. Even on the sunniest days, it was densely shadowed. The black iron poles of the fence were all askew, held together only by ropelike vines. The cemetery ground was bumpy, full of rocks, and crowded with rows of sunken tombstones covered with moss. The lopsided markers seemed to be marching in rows over the uneven ground. Noochum was nowhere in sight. Soon the field that bordered the cemetery was before me, and just beyond, at the bottom of the hill, were the whitewashed houses of Big Komjaty.

"We made it," I whispered into the basket, and broke into a run. But the motion upset the chicken, and it began to cackle from fright. I stopped running and again calmed her down.

When I got to the busy yard of the *shochet*, women, girls, and boys were hurrying in and out carrying their Sabbath dinners. Geese, ducks, and chickens went in alive and came out dead. I stood at the gate for a few minutes and watched the people greeting each other with "Have a good Sabbath." Then I remembered Babi's warning not to linger, and I ran inside the low building toward the slaughterer and handed him the basket.

The *shochet*, a very tall and slender man, was dressed in black silk from head to toe. His white collar and socks matched his white cheeks and long hands. He was young, and his dark beard, with full sidelocks, covered his jaws. He stood behind a trough that was splattered with blood. Above his head some chickens hung by their feet from hooks, waiting to be picked up. The swishing of shoes in the sawdust on the floor was the only sound in the room except for the slaughterer's voice as he recited the ritual prayer in a low monotone. As soon as he took the frightened chicken out of my basket and reached for his sharp knife, I lost my nerve and started to run out, but his voice caught me at the door. "Come back in a few minutes." When I returned he handed me the basket with the now dead chicken and said, "Have a good Sabbath."

I turned, walked back through the courtyard, and started my journey home to Babi's. But this time as I walked toward the cemetery, I spotted Noochum perched on the iron gate. He was twice the size of any rooster I had ever seen.

The encounter I had dreaded was less than one hundred meters away, with no possibility of avoiding it in sight, if I wanted to go home. Now I didn't even have a chicken to talk to. I just stood where I was and waited, hoping he'd go away. But even if he flew away and I could not see him, how could I be sure he would not jump out at me from some hiding place? I decided I would have to wait until someone came along. I stood there for a long time; my stomach began to growl from hunger, and I realized it must be past noon. But even such a familiar and natural sensation was startling in these circumstances, and I was sure that in some way Noochum was responsible for the growling in my stomach. Maybe this was his way of casting a spell.

I was growing frantic when a peasant woman finally came along, carrying two large jugs of water hanging from a yoke on her broad shoulders. Clouds of dust rose around her chunky ankles and bare feet as she mechanically half shuffled and half walked under the weight of the jugs.

When she came up to where I was standing, I started to walk slowly alongside her, keeping her between me and the cemetery. I looked toward her, hoping for a comforting word, but instead her rude, sarcastic voice was so loud I was sure that Noochum could hear. "Are you afraid of the cemetery?" she asked.

"No."

"What do you have in the basket?"

"A chicken."

"Did you kill it?"

"No."

"Did you have it killed?"

"Yes." I wished she would stop talking about all this killing.

"I kill my own chicken when I decide to cook one," she continued.

"We are not allowed to kill our own."

"Oh, you must be a *djidka*," she said, using the Ukrainian word for Jewess. "You have some strange customs. By the time you get that chicken home, it will stink."

"There is this rooster . . ." I said as we were nearing the cemetery gate, and I was sorry at once for mentioning him. Noochum was looking right at us. Except for his shriveled pink face, he was all black, and his brown-yellow eyes, like amber beads stuck into his loose-hanging flesh, were focused on the two of us.

"Oh, someone told you about him," the peasant woman said, trying to read my thoughts. "That is the truth they told you. But he doesn't bother us Christians. He just works his spells on the Jews. Have you done anything to upset him?"

"No."

"Then you shouldn't be scared." She went close to the gate, leaving me on the other side of the road, and shooed the rooster into flight. His large wings made a loud flapping noise. The woman started shaking with laughter as she alternately looked at the rooster and at me. Noochum's wings picked up momentum, stirring up great swirls of dust as he crowed in loud protest and circled in front of her. Her laughter became hysterical cackling, blending with Noochum's cries. As the laughter shook her body, water spilled out of her jugs, each splash sending up its own puff of dust to blend with the cloud Noochum's wings were beating into the air.

I started running down the hill, the dead chicken bouncing around in the basket on my arm. I glanced back over my shoulder into the bright rays of the sun and saw Noochum and the billowing dust cloud, seemingly flecked with sparks—almost flamelike—in the afternoon glare. I kept running until finally the pounding of my heart filled my ears and drowned out the sound of the cackling.

When I reached Babi's house, she was standing in the road, shielding her eyes from the sun with a cupped hand, looking for me. "I was getting worried," she said, taking the basket as she quickly moved her eyes over my face and body. "You are trembling. Did anything happen?" She didn't wait for an answer, but continued, "I have to hurry and pluck the chicken, or I won't have time to cook it before sundown. Come, have your lunch while I work, and tell me what happened."

I felt as limp as the chicken Babi pulled out of the basket. "I am not hungry. Would it be all right if I cooled off in the rain barrel?" I asked.

Babi was a little taken aback, but then, still holding the chicken, she looked me over, shrugged her shoulders, and said, "Sure, why not? Go, *shaefele*, wash away whatever is troubling you."

The Ducks

Tercsa lived across the road from Babi. She had a limp and her lame foot was supported by a high-laced black orthopedic shoe with a six-centimeter heel. On her other foot she wore a low oxford. Each made a different thump as it contacted the hard clay of her yard, sounding to me like the steps of two different people. During the summer, her son and daughter-in-law, who lived with her, worked out in the fields from dawn until sunset, and they usually took their two little girls with them. Tercsa kept busy with the household chores and tending the pigs, chickens, ducks, and geese. She yearned for companionship, but summer was a busy time in Komjaty, and nobody stopped to socialize except on Sundays. Tercsa felt left out of things, staying by herself six days a week.

Sometimes when I was alone because Babi was working in her own fields, Tercsa would call me over from our yard to sit and talk with her while she did her work. Besides taking care of the animals and cooking the meals, she also had to gather the hemp that was drying in the sun and beat it through her primitive thresher until the outside husks became brittle and broke off, leaving the fiber tangled like matted hair. Next she drew the fiber through a large mounted brush made out of spikes. After this long and tedious procedure, she tied the combed fiber onto her spindle. This was the part I liked best. By moistening the thumb and the forefinger of her right hand with saliva, she twisted several strands of the soft fiber into thread. Her left hand held a large, mushroom-shaped spool that was in constant motion winding up the freshly spun thread. Sitting on her stool behind the spindle, Tercsa herself became a machine, with both hands occupied in different movements and her good foot pedaling.

After letting me try her spindle, she set up a child-sized version of it for my use. At first, I got very frustrated because my thread was so uneven. Tercsa's was smooth and tight, almost like store-bought thread. Mine went in and came out in different thicknesses and became unraveled. Tercsa's old and patient hands then guided mine, and the thread started to even out. After I spun a satisfactory spool, she told me that when I visited Komjaty during the winter, her loom would be set up and she would teach me to weave the flax into homespun.

One Sunday, her son, Ivan, and his family had gone to visit his wife's family in a nearby village. Tercsa saw me in Babi's yard and asked me to come over and keep her company. She was as fascinated with my life in the modern city as I was with the traditions of the country. She could never hear enough about my city life, especially about the train I took from my house in Beregszász to Komjaty. That day she heard the train whistle in the distance and asked, "Aren't you scared of it?"

"Not at all. Why should I be?"

"Because it is driven by the devil."

"No, Tercsa, it has a furnace and the man on the train keeps shoveling in coal."

"Don't you believe it, child. It is the devil himself who drives that monster."

"Oh, Tercsa, have Ivan take you over to the train stop in the oxcart sometime so you can see the train for yourself."

"Not me, child. I don't ride on anything. I only go to places where my lame leg can take me."

"Well, the train is run by an engine that is heated by a furnace. If you had a furnace in your spindle, you would not have to move your arms; the heat of the coals would move things for you. I saw it and my stepfather explained it to me."

"What does this furnace look like?"

"It looks like a large stove."

"That's just what I thought. Now you explain this. How come I feed my stove coal and, thank the Lord Jesus, it doesn't go jumping off anywhere? If it moved just a finger's distance, you would hear me scream and yell until the saints came to rescue me. No, child, I am an old woman, I haven't gone out of Komjaty in my whole life, but I know this much. You can feed coal or wood to a stove—or a furnace—from now until the dead rise up and it won't go running, screaming, or whistling through the mountains like that black thing you call a train."

On this final note, Tercsa dismissed me. "Go home now, and let me finish cooking my beans for Sunday dinner before the evening church bells sound."

While Babi and I were eating our dinner on the porch, we heard Tercsa screaming as if she was in pain. We came running into her yard, where she had been cooking in a cauldron set on an iron triangle over a small fire of split wood. She was running around the fire hunched over, pounding her babushka-clad head with both fists.

"Tercsa, what happened?" asked Babi, running in step with Tercsa, trying to catch her and stop her.

"My beans, go look at them."

"What about them?"

"Go look for yourself."

Babi bent over the big iron pot, straining to see in the dusk. "I can't see anything," she said, picking up a large spoon and stirring the mixture.

"Good God, you are blind!" Tercsa screamed as she dropped her hands to her sides and looked up at the sky.

"You better stop screaming and show me. You're gathering a crowd."

"Let them come, let them see what happens to a poor

woman's beans just because I cooked them a few minutes past the church bells. They've all turned to blood. Come," she called to the people who had gathered at the gate, "you can all see."

Babi took hold of Tercsa's shoulders. "Tercsa, there is nothing wrong with your beans. It is not blood that you see. It's just the water, turned brown from the shells of the beans. You must have forgotten to rinse them."

"Don't tell me what I see. I see blood," said Tercsa, and she tore herself out of Babi's grasp. Before anybody could stop her, she picked up the heavy cast-iron pot and flung its contents over the expanse of the yard.

Babi and I returned to our half-eaten dinner. I was upset and confused about what I had seen. Babi offered to tell me a story about Tercsa to cheer me up and help me understand her better.

"In the days when her son, Ivan, was first married to Maria, he liked to take a drink now and then. Tercsa, being a very religious woman, was against alcohol, because their priest preached in his sermons about the evils of consuming alcohol and Tercsa lived by those sermons. She had some awful fights with Ivan over his drinking.

"So Ivan started to hide his bottle. One morning, after he'd had more to drink than he could handle the night before, Tercsa found his bottle in the hayloft, took it, and, without thinking, emptied it into the animals' water trough.

"Later in the day, her ducks were wobbling around the

yard, just barely able to walk. She picked a few of them up, examined them, and tried to feed them bread soaked in milk, but their limp bodies just rolled off her lap. Soon they were collapsed all over her yard. Poor Tercsa was beside herself with fright. What could have happened to the ducks? What would Ivan and Maria say when they came home to find all the ducks dead? She decided to pluck them to save their feathers at least, and to hide the dead bodies for the time being.

"She was putting the feathers away when Ivan came home early from the fields and found the whole flock of bare ducks wobbling about the yard. He thought that Tercsa had gone completely mad, and he started to scream at her. She just screamed back at him. Soon their yard filled up with neighbors like me and passersby who laughed at the spectacle of the naked ducks. They all wanted to know how this happened.

"Tercsa, now feeling very righteous because the ducks were not dead, decided to use this incident to cure Ivan of his drinking habit. 'All right,' she declared for all of us to hear, 'take a good look at my ducks and then I'll tell you what brought them to this sad state. But, Ivan, you'll have to promise me'—and she wagged a finger at him—'that you will never take another drop of alcohol in your life.'

"Poor Ivan was on the spot; everyone was looking at him. He knew that his mother liked to show what a strict hold she kept on him, so he just shrugged what looked like an 'all right,' wanting the whole scene to be over with.

"'You promise?' Tercsa questioned, and continued without waiting for an answer. 'Well, I found your bottle hidden in the hayloft and, not thinking because I was so mad . . . Well, anyway, some of your alcohol got into the water trough and the ducks must have gone over and drunk it. Then, later, I saw them wobbling around. I tried to feed them bread, but that didn't work and they collapsed all over the yard. Holy Mother of God, I thought, they are all dying and here I am, an old woman alone; what am I to do? I decided to pluck their feathers. It was better to have the feathers than nothing, and I cried as I felt their little bodies still warm against my legs. I filled up a sack with feathers and went to put it in the attic. Then I heard you in the yard and suddenly realized what had made the poor things sick—your alcohol.'"

Babi stopped her story at this point with a strange expression on her face, a mix of amusement and sadness.

"What happened to the ducks?" I asked.

"They eventually grew new feathers."

"What about Ivan? Did he drink after that?"

"I'm really not sure. But he will always remember that incident."

I did not find this story comforting after what I had just witnessed. I said to Babi, "I'm not going to visit Tercsa anymore. It was scary."

"Why did you go today?" Babi asked.

"Because she was lonely."

"Do you think that she will be less lonely after this?"

"I don't like her anymore. She acted just like a witch and she believes in the devil."

"Do you believe in witches?"

"No, but I have heard about them in stories."

"Well, Tercsa heard about the devil in stories. You need to be patient, Piri. Tercsa acts the way she does because she is lonely and wants attention, which is something we all need from time to time."

The Robbery

After my grandfather died, I had many lengthy discussions with Babi about death, burials, and souls, which caused me to have nightmares. I dreamed about the lopsided tombstones in the old cemetery sinking into the ground and my not being able to find my grandfather's grave. Each night I could hear his voice repeatedly calling my name. I would lie motionless, half awake, soaked in sweat, unable to move, waiting for dawn to enter the darkness of the room I slept in with Babi. One of the hardest things to get used to in the country was the pitch darkness of the night. Without electricity and streetlights, everything was covered in a black veil, except on moonlit nights.

When I confided to Babi that I was afraid to go to sleep, instead of the warm milk she usually gave me, she started brewing me a mixture of her dried herbs, adding some of the chamomile flowers that we had picked together. She made me drink the strong aromatic tea before going to sleep.

"This will make you dream of the meadows where we picked these flowers," she promised. Sure enough, my nightmares became less frequent.

Then, on one of those black, moonless nights when, as Babi would say, "you can't see your hand before your eyes," I was awakened from a deep sleep. I opened my eyes in the middle of a silent scream, not sure if the man's silhouette I saw rushing past my bed was part of a nightmare or a real prowler. Listening intently and searching the dark room, I heard strange sounds. It made me sit up with a start in my little bed. My first thought was to run to Babi's bed across the room, but I was too afraid. I lay back down and pulled the cover over my head instead, leaving only a small opening for my mouth, and whispered, "Babi, are you asleep? I think somebody is in the house."

"You must have had one of your bad dreams, Piri. I'll light the lamp."

I sneaked a peek from under the covers and saw Babi get out of bed. I could just make out her long white nightdress of homespun cloth and ruffled cap as she moved to her night table in the darkness.

"Piri," she called, "did you take my matches from the night table?"

"No, Babi. I didn't take the matches."

"They're gone. You know how I always put them on the night table before I go to bed in case I wake up in the night and need to light the lamp. I clearly remember putting them there last night. Someone must have taken them. What did you say woke you up, child, what did you hear?"

Now Babi's voice sounded scared. She turned to walk toward me. When she reached my bed I whispered, "Babi, I'm pretty sure I saw someone in here, and heard strange noises, too."

Babi switched from Yiddish to Ukrainian as she tiptoed passed my bed into the kitchen. "Whoever dares to enter an old woman's house better be prepared to face the wrath of God as well as the police!"

Babi came back with a box of long matches. She struck one and lit the kerosene lamp on her night table. Continuing to speak in Ukrainian, she held the lamp up over her shoulder and started walking around, peering into the shadowy corners of our room. "Where are you hiding, you coward?" she said.

Babi looked very small in her long white nightdress. Her felt slippers were silent on the dirt floor, and the flame of her lamp barely lit the space she moved in. The rest of the room remained dark. Outside the small windows it was still pitch-black, and it had started to rain.

Babi stopped in the middle of the room for a few seconds and listened. Hearing no sound or movement but the rain, she became convinced that whoever it was had since fled. She seemed more upset now than frightened as she sat down on my bed and spoke to me in Yiddish. "I'm sure you are right, Piri. Someone must have been in here. I think I heard something, too. I thought it was the cat."

As Babi got up and headed toward the pantry, which was at one end of our bedroom, she hiked up her nightdress with her free hand before stepping over the high threshold. Not wanting to be left alone, and fearing for Babi, I got out of bed and stood behind her. The pantry door, which she insisted on keeping closed so the cat could not go in and help himself to food, was ajar. Babi walked right in. I stopped, too scared to take another step.

I heard Babi cry out, "Oh no!" and I rushed to her side. Peering over her hunched figure as she lowered the kerosene lamp almost to the floor, I saw a large hole dug in the outside wall, big enough for a grown man to crawl through. We could look into the vegetable garden and watch the rain pound the ground. There was rumbling thunder, followed by lightning.

"Babi, let's go back in the bedroom," I pleaded, but she stopped only long enough to ask me to recite a Hebrew prayer with her. It was a special prayer for lightning. It didn't comfort me in the least. I stood in my nightgown hugging myself, shivering from the damp cool air, and from fright.

Babi finally straightened up and asked, "Piri, did you see anything, any strangers around here yesterday?" She only paused for a second before answering herself, "No, of course you didn't. You're never around the house. You're always off roaming about with your friend Molcha."

Now I knew how upset Babi was because she sounded angry with me, and paid no attention to how scared I was. I got out of her way, but then Babi took a step and hit her head on the top shelf, where she stored dairy products in glazed clay pottery. The covered butter dish fell over her shoulder, crashing on the hard dirt floor. The sound of the crash scared the cat out of his hiding place and he jumped over Babi's hunched back. We both screamed. Babi, thrown off balance, barely managed to steady the kerosene lamp in her hands.

Now she was more upset than I had ever seen her. She turned her anger on Paskudniak—Mr. Ugly, the cat. As usual, she addressed him in Ukrainian, the language she used for *goyim*, anyone who wasn't Jewish. When I first asked Babi why she spoke to him in Ukrainian, she had explained that Jews don't hunt and kill animals, so the cat wasn't Jewish and wouldn't understand Yiddish. Now she called Paskudniak stupid, sneaky, a thief, and a murderer of birds and other unsuspecting creatures. Then, switching back to Yiddish, Babi looked at me and said, "Do you realize that this ugly thing almost made me burn down the house? If I had dropped the lamp . . ."

The cat meowed softly; he clearly understood Babi's anger at him. They had lived together a long time. He came to my side and brushed against my ankles. I felt his old, sagging body quiver, and it made me realize that he was as scared as we were. I didn't dare pick him up or even pet him, knowing how angry Babi was at both of us.

"Should I put him out?"

"What good would it do?" Babi snapped, pointing to the big hole in the wall, as she stooped to pick up some of the larger pieces of broken pottery, and tried to salvage some of the butter. "He will come right back in here and gorge himself until he gets sick. Then we'll have to clean that up. No, we'd best keep him inside with us and close the pantry door."

The cat followed us into the bedroom, but stayed near me. His long tail was usually curled up, but now it was dragging, limp as a rope, on the dirt floor. He continued sulking until I sneaked him a pat. He responded with gentle meows and crawled under my bed. I hesitated, then said, "I wish we had a key to lock the bedroom door."

"Don't worry, it is unlikely that the robber will come back. No, he is long since gone . . . He probably got away before the rain started."

Babi put the lamp back on the night table, and opened the double doors of her wardrobe. It was a massive piece of dark mahogany furniture, placed on the wall across from Babi's bed. It was fitted with shelves on the right and poles for hangers on the left, and two drawers stretched from side to side on the bottom. It served as both a wardrobe and a linen closet, and from fall to spring Babi stored quince on top. This hardy fruit provided an important addition to Babi's numerous apple compotes and, best of all, it filled the room with the pungent yet delicate aroma unique to quince.

Babi was standing on tiptoe in front of the open wardrobe. I got her a chair so she could reach the top shelf, She stepped up on it and searched the shelf. "Dear God, my box is gone! What would anyone want with my burial garments?" she cried. Now she was practically in tears.

Babi got down from the chair and searched between the tablecloths on the second shelf. "He must have taken my money, too! It could not have been a stranger. It had to be someone who knows where I keep these things."

Babi turned suddenly, as if something had just occurred to her. She picked up the lamp and headed toward the kitchen. I hurried to keep up with her so I would not be left in the dark.

The rain continued to wash over the small kitchen window like a black curtain. Then there was a loud boom that practically shook the house. A momentary flash of jagged light entered the kitchen, lighting up Babi's face. Catching her breath, she said, "It sounded as if the lightning hit a tree in the forest. I hope it won't cause a fire. We better repeat the prayer."

Standing in the kitchen with Babi, I realized that what had awakened me was not the man in the room but the jingling of the *pushke*, the container in which Babi collected money for the poor. We both looked at the shelf by the oven where it was kept and said in unison, "It's gone."

Babi held up the lamp and looked around the rest of the kitchen, but nothing else seemed to be missing. We returned to the bedroom. Babi sat down on her bed and dangled her feet over the edge. I climbed up next to her and crawled under the covers. I was still shivering from cold and fright.

"Do you remember Yani coming here to borrow an umbrella?"

I did not remind her that I had been with Molcha, who lived across the road, because I could tell that Babi was thinking out loud.

"I thought it was strange; I remember wondering, since when does a farm boy need an umbrella? Yani said that he was going to the fair in Szölös and it looked like rain. He was right about the rain; I hope it will stop by morning. I did not want to refuse him. It would be hard to believe that a boy I watched grow up would want to rob me." Babi's voice grew reminiscent and sad. "And how could someone have dug that hole? He must have done it while I was in the fields, but I never lock my doors, certainly not during the day. He could have just walked right in instead. It just doesn't make sense!"

Babi finally got under the covers too. I curled around her. It gradually stopped raining, and an eerie quiet settled over us. I could hear the cat snoring under my bed.

"It will soon be light," Babi said, turning to face me. "You will have to go and get the police. I'll stay here and watch everything."

"Should I tell them about the hole or what he took?"

"Just tell them that your grandmother wants them to come immediately. The less said, the better. I'll tell them the rest when they get here."

"Will you tell them about Yani?"

"I don't know yet, but don't you mention it."

We did not go back to sleep. We got up at the first sign of dawn, and after I had my breakfast, I went to get the police. I knew where the police station was, but when I got there, I was scared to go in. I tried to rehearse what I would say. I knew that I had to say enough to persuade them to come, but not too much or Babi would be mad at me. I had a habit of being talkative, especially when I was nervous. I took a deep breath and pulled the string on the bell.

A gruff man's voice called, "Come in," and my heart began to pound. I pushed the heavy door open and saw a policeman sitting next to a stove drinking coffee from a large earthenware mug. He wiped drops of coffee off his mustache with the back of his hand, and asked, "What have we here?"

Another policeman and a man in civilian clothes appeared and strode to the middle of the room. With all three of them staring at me, I felt like turning around and running, but I knew better.

"I came to report a robbery. My grandmother sent me. She asked that you come right away to see it. I mean, to have her tell you all about it."

The man sitting next to the stove said, "Why don't you tell us about it? You're a clever city girl, aren't you?"

I looked down at my dress and boots. Babi had told me to wear one of my smart school dresses and my new rubber boots. I could feel my face turn red.

"You're doing well," the other policeman said. He took a step toward me to encourage me. "Who is your grandmother?"

"Her name is Mrs. Fage Rosner."

"I know who she is," said the man at the stove, lighting his pipe. "She is the old widow who lives in Little Komjaty. She has sons in America and they send her money. I've seen her a couple of times at the post office when she comes to pick it up."

"Did the robber steal her money?" the policeman asked.

"I'm not supposed to say anything, just ask you to come." The three of them exchanged looks and chuckled.

The man at the stove said, "You two go on, the old lady does pay her taxes. I'll stay and wait for the next case." They chuckled again.

Then the three of us started the long walk back. The policeman asked me, "Why does your grandmother want to live here?"

"She has always lived here. She doesn't like the city. She likes the country, her animals, and the farm. She hardly ever leaves the farm. My mother would like her to come and live with us, especially since my grandfather died, but she is very set in her ways."

I was going to say more, but remembered what Babi had said—"The less said, the better."

Babi was waiting for us, and she and I led them into the house and showed them the hole in the pantry wall. The policeman started to question Babi, and the man in civilian clothes took out a notebook and a short pencil from his pocket to take down all the information.

"You live here by yourself?" the policeman asked.

"My granddaughter is staying with me," said Babi, putting her hands on my shoulders. The man who was writing shook his head.

"Rosner, that's Jewish, right?"

Babi dropped her hands from my shoulders. "Yes, I'm Jewish, what does that have to do with it?"

"Well, nothing much, but with you living here all alone among the Christians, something like this was bound to happen."

I heard the anger in Babi's voice as she replied, "I've lived here all my life. I was born in this house. I watched that boy grow up."

"What boy?"

Babi sighed deeply. "It's just as well, I guess I would have told you anyway. Yesterday Yani came by. He said he was going to the fair in Szölös and it looked like rain. He came to ask me for an umbrella."

"An umbrella? I did not know anybody here owned an umbrella," said the policeman, turning to look at the other man. They both laughed.

"Well, he knew I had one, but that was just an excuse to get in and look over the house, I think. He stayed and talked for a while."

"Did he go to Szölös?"

"I don't know, but he was right about the rain."

"You'll have to give me his name and tell me where he lives."

"Yani lives diagonally to the right, just past that field," said Babi, pointing down the road in the direction of Yani's house.

"And his last name?"

"Kolovani. Yani Kolovani."

Babi put her hands on my shoulders again. The man who had been writing put away his notebook and the two men started to walk toward the door.

"We'll let you know if we find out anything, and if anything turns up here, you come and let us know," said the policeman.

"Do you think it was him?" Babi asked.

"It is pretty dangerous to make accusations unless you are sure. Living the way you do, I would be very careful."

They walked out, leaving Babi angry. She turned back toward the kitchen, muttering to herself. "I don't need them. I will know who the robber was."

"How, Babi? How will you know?"

"I'll know because whoever steals a *pushke* and uses the money that was meant for charity will die before the year is out. That is what they say," said Babi, waving a hand in the direction of the shelf that held her prayer books.

I trembled at the thought, not doubting its truth for a moment, because Babi had said it. I hoped it would turn out to be someone else. "Please don't let it be Yani," I prayed in silence.

I remembered the times Babi had gone over to the *pushke* and dropped coins in before lighting the Sabbath candles, if someone was sick, or taking a journey. Whenever there was apprehension, giving money to the poor was a way of asking for a blessing. At home I would put some of my coins in our *pushke* if I had done something wrong like skipping religious school, telling a lie, or wishing a curse on someone. Putting the coins in never failed to make me feel better.

Days passed and we heard nothing from the police. Nor did Yani appear to return the umbrella. Babi said no more about the robbery or about the box containing her burial clothes. We carried on with our routines of work and play. Babi did not seem to be thinking about what had happened.

Then, after a few weeks, we heard that Yani was sick with a high fever. I could see that Babi was upset when she heard about it.

"Is he going to die?" I asked.

"Shush," said Babi. "You mustn't . . ."

"But the police didn't find anyone else."

Babi waved her hand. "The police! I'm sure they forgot about it as soon as they left here. Why do they care about an old woman like me? They almost accused me, as if I asked for this by living in my own house."

I could hear Babi repeatedly questioning the farmers who came by about Yani. "Has his fever broken? Did his chills stop?" But she did not go over and visit and help as she usually did when one of the farmers was sick.

Yani's fever did not break, and finally a doctor was sent for from a neighboring village. But it was too late. Babi and I were on the porch in the evening when we heard wailing coming from the direction of their house.

"Come, let's go inside," said Babi, and as we walked into the house, she turned and locked the heavy oak door behind us.

I was sitting on the porch the next day when I saw Yani's mother on the road. She wore a black dress, shoes, babushka, and shawl. I was startled to see her walking toward our gate. She looked so determined that I was afraid to let her into the house.

"Is your grandmother inside?" she asked, and was in the kitchen before I could answer. Babi laid her prayer book aside and jumped up from her chair to meet her. Yani's mother was a large woman and she looked even bigger dressed as she was. Babi's tiny frame was practically hidden by her. I walked around her and stood beside Babi.

As we faced her, Yani's mother opened her shawl and took a white box from under her arm. Extending it to Babi, she said, "I found this in our attic. I hope you will find it in your heart to pray for the boy, Fage, and let his soul rest. This was not like him. Yani was a good boy."

Babi took the box, set it down on the kitchen table, opened it, and quickly went through the contents. "My burial clothes are intact," she said. "I'm grateful for that. I am very sorry for your loss, Marya. I will pray for Yani and for you. His soul will rest. I am a mother, too. I understand your pain."

After Yani's mother left, Babi sat down, her shoulders sagging.

"Are you sure that Yani died because he stole the *pushke*?" I asked.

Babi waved her arms toward the shelf that held her prayer books and answered in a sad voice, "That's what they say. It must be God's will."

The Beggar Woman

There were beggars in Babi's village, but only one was a woman. Her name was Bracha, but many people just called her the Beggar Woman. Her face resembled a wintered-over potato. She wore a dark kerchief tightly knotted under her chin. She dressed in raggedy hand-me-downs and the color of her dress was too faded to be distinguishable. She always wore an unbuttoned black men's coat, regardless of the weather. Her ankle-high shoes were laced up to the first three sets of holes because her ankles were too puffy to fit in the confined space. Bracha's mouth was in perpetual motion, but she hardly ever spoke.

On Fridays, when all the Jewish families were preparing to welcome the Sabbath, she would stop at every Jewish home and stand motionless in their doorways until she was acknowledged and handed a coin. Late one Friday afternoon when I was helping Babi make our Sabbath dinner, she arrived and stood silently on the stoop in the frame of the kitchen door. I turned to Babi. She looked up expectantly and greeted her, "Good Sabbath, Bracha."

Babi motioned for me to get things for Bracha to wash her hands with. I took the soap dish, a water cup, and a towel from the kitchen and led Bracha to the well in the front yard. She followed me in silence. I could hear her flat shoes shuffling behind me on the dirt path. Some of the chickens pecking in the grass stopped to watch her as we passed. I handed Bracha the soap, scooped water over her hands from the water bucket until all the dirt was washed away, and gave her the towel. She never looked up at me. I returned to the kitchen while Bracha waited on the porch.

I put a soup bowl on top of a dinner plate and walked to the stove, where Babi stood with the ladle in her hand. Holding the plate steady, I watched the steaming golden broth glide from the ladle into the bowl. Then Babi put some of her finely cut homemade noodles in the soup. I balanced the plate and was about to go to the porch when Babi called me back and, as an afterthought, added a piece of chicken. I stopped at the high stoop and watched Bracha walk to the table on the porch outside our kitchen door and take her place on the bench.

I had never dared to take a close look at Bracha. But this Friday she glanced up at me as I put the plate down for her. Her eyes were cloudy, covered with a milky veil. Her brown face was lumpy. She smelled of the country, all of it—the bitter and sour grasses, the wild mushrooms, the

43

roasted acorns people in Komjaty made coffee from, and the farm animals.

Bracha looked at her soup and began to eat. Her hands trembled in the same constant motion as her mouth. I wondered if she kept them hidden in her coat sleeves because she didn't want us to see them shake. Somehow she managed to guide the spoon to her mouth without spilling much of the soup. When she finished, Babi came out and placed a piece of her challah and two short candles on the table and said, "Go home, Bracha, and light your candles; the sun is starting to set."

Bracha slid off the bench, shook out her dirty dress, dropped the challah and the candles in one of the deep pockets of her skirt, faced Babi, and, stuttering barely audible words, said, "May you be blessed."

Babi put a hand on Bracha's shoulder, guiding her to the road.

I was full of questions, but Babi's concentration was set on the Sabbath. She walked right past me into the kitchen. I followed behind her and asked, "Doesn't Bracha have any family?"

"No questions until we finish all we have to do to welcome the Sabbath."

"But—"

"Piri, I said no questions until we finish our preparations."

Babi's face was set, her hands busy, as she kept looking

out the kitchen doorway at the sinking sun. I finished setting the table, and waited for her to come. She finally took off her apron, folded it, and let out a sigh of relief. She walked to the table, covered her head with her white lace scarf, and lit the candles. Next, she ceremoniously circled her arms over the flames of the candles three times. Then she cupped her hands over her face and whispered the special prayer for lighting the Sabbath candles. She asked for God's blessings for her children and their families, and for peace among men, and said a special blessing to keep Jerusalem safe. During our dinner I kept my need to ask questions inside me and instead complimented Babi on the delicious Sabbath meal, even though I preferred my mother's more seasoned cooking.

Not until the dinner dishes were cleared away did Babi finally sit down and ask, "Piri, what was that you were asking about Bracha?"

"I wanted to know if she has any family."

"No, she doesn't. She was married for a short time to a much older man, a widower with two grown daughters. It didn't work out. The girls took advantage of her and the man couldn't make a decent living. So Bracha left and moved back in with her aging parents, and she looked after them until they passed away. She lives alone in their house now. Bracha is not as feeble-minded as most people think. She must have learned along the way that silence can be the best answer. I remember when we were in school, she would sometimes surprise the teacher with what she said."

"You went to school with her?"

"Yes, but our school was not like the one you have in the city. The schoolhouse we went to was even smaller than what we have here today. We used slate boards to write on instead of paper. We had one teacher and she had to teach all ages. Bracha and I are only a couple of years apart."

"But she looks ancient!"

"That's what loneliness and neglect does to us."

"Was she like this when she was young or could she speak?"

"She always had a speech problem, like a stutter. Now she also has the trembling sickness. Many old people get that."

"Did the children make fun of her when she was young?"

"They did. They called her stupid, and worse."

"Were you friends with her then, even though the other children called her names?"

"Especially *because* they were cruel to her. Bracha needed a friend."

"Did the other children still play with you after you became her friend?"

"Some did and some did not, but it didn't bother me. The ones that were so mean to her were not worth bothering about. Why would I want such mean friends? Also, because I was an only child, I understood what it was like to be lonely. My mother liked Bracha. She told me that I could bring her home anytime. I knew she would not have liked me bringing home some of the other children who weren't nice."

Listening to Babi, I understood that what she did was very generous and kind, and also very brave. But I did not think that I could do it. My friend Molcha and I had often seen children teasing Bracha. She never answered them. She just waved her arms as if she were chasing flies and kept on walking.

"Molcha and I have seen the village children tease her," I said.

"Children, like adults, always look for scapegoats to make them feel superior," Babi said. "It is a mean trait in human nature. Those children probably learn this from their parents and know that they can tease Bracha. But, Piri, do you think that watching and feeling sorry when somebody teases her helps her in any way?"

"Babi, what can we do? We can't stop them; they would never listen to us. There are many of them and they are very big. If we tell on them, they are sure to come after us. Molcha's brother once tried to stand up to them and they called him an albino because of his white skin and hair."

"You or Molcha should run to an adult for help, but one of you should also stay there to make sure Bracha is okay."

———

After what Babi said about Bracha needing a friend, I started to greet her whenever I passed her on the road. Then one Friday morning when Babi sent me with a chicken to the *shochet* for our Sabbath dinner, I had to walk right past her house. She lived just down the hill from the Jewish cemetery. I noticed that Bracha kept a goat in her back yard. As I was returning from the slaughterer with the dead chicken in my basket, I put down the basket to rest my arm.

I heard a big commotion ahead of me, but I couldn't see what it was because the road curved and there was a cornfield in the way. I crossed the field to see what was going on. As I walked between the cornstalks I saw some boys running through the field. When I saw who they were, I turned around and ran back to get my basket and go straight home. But as I reached the road, I had barely taken a few steps when I saw Bracha lying on the ground. She was not moving. She looked dead. I remembered what Babi said—that if Bracha was in trouble, either Molcha or I should stay with her while the other one went for help. But I was alone.

As I was trying to decide what to do, I saw a man on an oxen wagon coming toward me. I ran to meet him. Only farmers used oxen wagons, but as I got close I saw that this man did not look like a farmer. Farmers were always brown from working in the fields, and this man's face was very white. Everyone in Komjaty knew that there were ghosts around the cemetery. I couldn't move. I stood there until the wagon reached me. The man wore farmer's clothes, which were covered with white dust. Even though I was afraid he was a ghost, I told him I needed help. He said, "You can't carry that basket?"

"No, it's not the basket. There's a dead woman lying in the road," I replied, sure he didn't believe me.

He said, "Okay, climb up. Show me. I know who you are. I know your grandmother; I've seen you there. You're a city girl, aren't you?"

I was afraid to answer him. So I just looked around in the wagon. I noticed that his hands holding the harness were as white as his face. He smiled as he looked at me, showing his teeth. But I still didn't believe that he wasn't a ghost.

"Where is the dead woman?"

"Over there."

As soon as we reached Bracha, we jumped out of the wagon. The farmer tried to move her, but she let out a cry. He picked her up under her arms and dragged her along on the heels of her shoes. He hoisted her up and laid her on the sacks of flour. She didn't open her eyes. I climbed up next to him.

"Where are you taking her?" I asked.

"I'm taking her to your grandmother. She will know what to do."

I hoped he was telling me the truth. I kept turning my head to look at Bracha. I now knew she was alive, but she hadn't moved a finger. When we got to Babi's house she was standing at the gate waiting for me. The driver stood up, pulling the reins tight to bring the oxen to a stop, and called to Babi, "I'm bringing you the Beggar Woman whom you are friendly with. Your granddaughter found her lying in the road."

Babi climbed up on the spokes of the wheel and looked into the wagon. Her face turned the color of ash.

"Help me bring her into the house," she said to the man.

He dragged her out of the wagon, once again gripping her under her limp arms. She looked like an overgrown rag doll. Babi tried to help him by holding Bracha by her feet. One of Bracha's shoes fell off, exposing a dirty foot. Babi called, "Piri, don't just stand there and stare. Hold open the door."

"Where do you want her?" the man asked.

Babi rushed ahead to the guest room, pulled a straw mattress out from under the bed, and called, "Bring her in here."

Dropped on the mattress, Bracha finally opened her eyes. Witnessing her reawakening, the man turned to Babi and said, "I'll leave you now. I have to get home."

Babi thanked him. Bracha tried to speak but was incoherent.

"Just rest," Babi said in her most reassuring voice. Turning to me, Babi asked what had happened.

"I don't know. I found her like this on the road."

"Did you see anything?"

"I saw some boys running through the cornfield."

"My God! Look at her neck," Babi said. "Somebody tried to choke her. She is hurt badly. I'll need some help. We have to take these dirty clothes off her and wash her wounds, and we have to—" Babi stopped mid-sentence, shaking her head from side to side. Turning back to me, she asked, "Where is the chicken?"

"I put the basket in the kitchen."

"Good. I'll make some soup." Still talking, Babi walked outside to the well, and I followed her. "I'll have to heat some water to wash Bracha. But I can't wash her by myself."

Babi turned around to look at me. I could tell she was deciding what to do next. "Piri," she said, "do you remember where the Gottlieb sisters live, the ones who came to wash Grandpa for his burial?"

"In between the seamstress's house and Bracha's house. I saw them there when you took me to try on my dress before the seamstress finished it."

"That's right. You'll have to go and tell them I want them to come here."

"But, Babi, they live so far."

"Never mind, I have nobody else to send and there's no one else who would want to do this."

"Is she going to die?"

"I don't know how badly she's hurt, but I hope not."

With this, Babi dismissed me and began drawing water from the well.

When I got to the Gottliebs' house, their door was ajar. I stood on their front step and could see both women in the kitchen chatting; they were busy preparing their Sabbath dinner. They didn't even notice me watching them. I stood for a while, not sure if I should speak and startle them, so I knocked on the outside of the door, pretending that I just got there.

"What do you want?" they asked.

I rushed inside to deliver Babi's message.

"Tell your grandmother that we can't do it. We have to finish cooking before it is time to light the Sabbath candles. She should know that. I bet she has her cooking all done."

"No she doesn't. I was late bringing home the chicken from the *shochet* on account of finding Bracha lying on the road. Babi wants you to help her wash Bracha."

"You better tell the truth. Is Bracha dead or almost dead? The burial society only pays us for bathing dead people. So is she dead?"

"No, but she probably will be by the time you get there," I said, trying to convince them it was urgent.

"Come and get us when she's dead."

"Babi told me not to come back without you."

"Oh, all right! Go tell her we'll come after we have finished making our dinner."

When I got home, Babi had the chicken soup boiling.

"How's Bracha?" I asked.

"She's resting for now," Babi said. "We'll wake her when the Gottlieb sisters get here."

When the Gottlieb sisters arrived, they went right to work taking her clothes off while Babi poured the hot water from the pots into a metal washtub. As they pulled her dirty dress over her head, we heard jingling coins streaming onto the dirt floor. All hands stopped as we watched in shocked surprise to see coins raining from her pockets in a torrent. This was a lot more than Bracha could beg for from families—I had never seen so many coins in one place.

I bent down to pick some up, but Babi scolded, "Just leave the money there for now. You mustn't handle money on the Sabbath."

"What happened to her neck?" one of the sisters asked.

"She told me some boys came and yanked her pouch off her neck. After that, she can't remember anything."

"This is quite a gouge," said one of the sisters.

Babi put her small hand under Bracha's neck as one of the sisters poured some warm soapy water from a pitcher over the wounds. Bracha let out a cry.

"We will be very gentle, but if we don't clean your wounds they will fester and then you will be in big trouble," Babi said. "I'll get some iodine."

Bracha moaned while the sisters patted her dry and put her in a clean nightshirt of Babi's. After the sisters left,

Babi fed her some chicken soup. Bracha looked up at Babi with gratitude and tried to say thank you, then fell into a deep sleep.

That night I was wide awake. My head was reeling from all the excitement of the day, so Babi let me crawl into bed with her. I cuddled into her arms and finally asked the question that had been bothering me. "Was the man with the wagon a ghost?"

"What a thing to say. God forbid!"

"Then why was he so white?"

"He was coming from the mill and was dusted with flour."

"But aren't there ghosts around the cemetery?"

"Ptui, ptui." Babi spat in the air to chase away any evil spirits that might be lurking and then said, "I'm not sure. But anyway, they wouldn't come out on the road in broad daylight. They would be blinded."

The following night Babi and I were awakened by frightening sounds coming from Bracha's room. We couldn't tell if she was crying, cursing, or just confused about where she was. Babi and I jumped out of our beds in the main room and almost knocked each other over crossing through the kitchen to get to the guest room.

Babi spoke to her in a hushed voice as if she were a baby. "Bracha, you must calm down. Everything is going to be all right if you just take a deep breath and tell us what is bothering you. Even a mother can't understand her child if she doesn't speak."

Bracha sniffed and her chest heaved as she made an effort to explain. Lifting her head slightly off the pillow, she made a circle with both hands around her injured neck as if she were putting on a necklace. Letting her head fall on the pillow, she went back to making those awful jumbled sounds again. Babi pulled up a chair and said, "We understand it has to do with your pouch, and I'm going to sit here until you can tell us what you are crying about, so we can all go back to sleep."

Finally, Babi could make some sense out of Bracha's grief and translated to me that Bracha's mother's wedding ring, as well as her own, and a brooch encrusted with precious stones that was also her mother's, had been in the pouch.

A couple of days later, a farmer brought the empty pouch to Babi's house. "This must belong to the Beggar Woman."

"Where did you find it?" Babi asked.

"In the cornfield near your cemetery. There was nothing in it," he replied defensively.

When the farmer left, Babi told me, "Those boys probably thought she kept coins in that pouch. They must have been very disappointed."

"Babi, why does she beg if she had so much money in her pockets?" I asked.

"This is one of her purposes in life, to collect money to take care of her parents' home. We all have different purposes, you know."

"I don't," I said, more to myself than to Babi.

"Yes, you do—otherwise you would not have been put on this earth. You just don't know what they are yet. You are too young. God will let you know when you are ready," Babi said with great conviction. I thought of all the possibilities, hoping that my mission would be nothing like Babi's, always needing to look after other people and animals, never having fun, always wearing dark, serious clothes, nothing with frills.

The next day the two Gottlieb sisters came to see how Bracha was doing. Zelda, the older of the two sisters, said to Babi, "Bracha can no longer live by herself. So my sister, Hanchi, and I have decided to have her live with us as soon as she recovers. We will take care of her, and she will be safe. Of course, she would have to pay us for room and board. We live on a small income."

Hearing those words, Bracha tried to sit up in bed in protest, but Babi held her back. In her stuttering voice Bracha explained, "I have to stay in my parents' house. I made a promise to them that I would take care of it."

"How can you take care of your house when you can't even take care of yourself?" Zelda said. "If it wasn't for Mrs. Rosner, you would be dead by now."

Babi protested, "I don't have it in my power to keep anybody alive; only the Almighty can do that. It just wasn't time for Bracha to go yet. Let's concentrate on getting her back on her feet first before we make any changes in her future."

Babi seemed to really enjoy taking care of Bracha and cooking up remedies for her. Every day she baked an onion and mashed it into a paste, adding several herbs that she pulverized with her mortar and pestle. She then placed the paste on Bracha's wounds, and it seemed to work, because they were healing. Bracha was regaining her strength, and her spirits lifted. As for Babi, I had not seen her as tirelessly occupied and pleased with what she was doing since Grandpa died.

By the end of the week Bracha could walk out to the porch, which was fragrant from the aroma of the ripening grapes that climbed along the sunny side, where Grandpa had originally planted them some twenty years before. She was no longer dirty but wearing clean clothes and slippers, and she sat on the bench like an invited, honored guest. Babi asked me to bring Bracha the footstool that Babi only used when she sat in her upholstered armchair reading her Bible or sewing. I don't believe it had ever been out of the house before. But by now I realized that many rules were being broken for her old friend Bracha. I began to resent Bracha and wished she would leave.

Bracha must have sensed that I resented her for taking Babi's attention away from me, and because Babi was keeping me in the house to help her instead of allowing me to play with Molcha or read my books. She gave me a twenty-five filler coin, but Babi made me give it back, explaining that we are not supposed to accept payment for a good deed. We are to be grateful that we are able to help the less fortunate, and we will be rewarded in good time.

The following Friday while Babi was making Sabbath dinner, Bracha said, "I have to go home and take care of my goat. She must be starving—soon she will dry up and stop giving milk."

Babi shook her head in annoyance. "I told you the Gottlieb sisters are taking good care of the goat."

"What about my house? It will fall apart from neglect."

"It wasn't in such good repair while you were there."

It was the first time I had heard Babi getting annoyed with Bracha. Bracha didn't know how seriously Babi took the preparation of the Sabbath.

Bracha's feelings were hurt. She went to her room, sat on the bed, and whimpered as she talked to herself. Babi continued assembling our dinner, and I finished setting the table. There was an extra set of candles prepared for Bracha to light and welcome the Sabbath.

After dinner, Babi sat with Bracha and said, "I'm sorry I was so sharp with you. You are right, it is time for you to go home, but you should really repair your house first. Especially your roof. You can afford it."

"My parents did leave me some money, but I don't want to put any more burden on you. You have already done too much. But the people who would do the work would not understand me—they would just laugh and turn me down."

"Nonsense, Bracha," Babi said. "I will help you."

On Sunday, Babi went to speak to the village's roof thatcher to ask him to mend Bracha's roof. She let me accompany her. We climbed the steep hill to Big Komjaty. As we walked past the Catholic cemetery, I held Babi's hand. It was dry. Once we had passed the cemetery, I dropped her hand. We entered a totally Christian neighborhood that I had never been to before. Men, women, and children were dressed in their Sunday best, clothes made of homespun cloth that was heavily embroidered. The men stood talking in separate clusters. The women sat on their porches. The children were running about playing, enjoying their day of rest. But as soon as they noticed us, all heads pivoted in our direction.

I felt like an intruder and reached for Babi's hand again, and this time it wasn't as dry.

"We shouldn't have come on a Sunday," I whispered.

"But during the week I am busy in the fields, and the thatcher might be in his fields or working on a roof and I wouldn't be able to find him."

One of the older men, who had graying hair, a generous mustache, and eyes as clear as the summer sky, walked toward us, addressed Babi as *Pani* Rosner, the Ukrainian equivalent for the word "Lady," and asked, "What brings you to our neighborhood?"

"I need your help. Not for myself, but for a friend, an old widow like myself. Her roof is leaking and she can't live in her house."

"I haven't been doing thatching these days. I'm getting too old for climbing the ladder. At best, I could supervise one of the younger men. Can she pay?"

"If the price is within reason."

"Where is the house?"

As Babi started to explain, a man in his late twenties joined us. "I know the house," he said, "but that woman died when she was robbed and beaten. Nobody has seen her since."

"That's because she has been staying with me. But now that she has recovered, she would like to go back to her house."

"You're talking about the Beggar Woman," commented the older man. "Where would she get the money to pay for it?"

Without thinking, I said, "They didn't take her money, because it wasn't in her pouch."

Babi gave my hand a strong squeeze of warning, but it was too late.

"So she has the money," said the older man, directing his question to me.

Babi answered in a rush, "Now that you know what house we are talking about, take a look at it and we'll talk money. You remember where I live?"

The young man volunteered, "I'll do the roof and I won't charge too much, knowing who it is for. I will pass by tomorrow and take a look to see how bad the damage is."

Within days everything was in full motion. Fresh straw

was delivered in an oxen wagon to Bracha's house, the Gottlieb sisters got caught up in the excitement and helped to clean up inside the house, and Bracha was so excited that she laughed and cried simultaneously. "Now I will have carried out my parents' wish to bring honor back to their house," she said, hugging Babi. "Thank you for arranging this for me. May you live to a hundred and twenty years and always be able to do God's work."

The following Sunday Babi decided to take Bracha to see the progress of her house. Bracha would not go during the week while the workers were there; she was too uncomfortable around people, especially *goyim*. So I asked Babi if Molcha and I could go for a walk along the Rika while they were gone. Babi gave me permission, and I ran across the road to see if Molcha could go with me.

At the river, there were several other children our age and younger splashing about between the large boulders in the running water. The adults sat under nearby trees with jugs and baskets of food. I had seen how the peasant women tied a knot in the front of their dresses to keep the skirts out of the way of the water, so I tied mine and Molcha's, too. Then I said, "We will stay in the shallow water, just deep enough to cool our feet."

As we got farther and farther away from the families who were picnicking, we saw two boys fighting. The bigger of the two was pushing the younger one down in the rushing water. I yelled at him to let go, but he kicked some water up at my face instead, soaking my dress.

Molcha stood petrified. I gave her a little push and sent her for help. She ran toward the trees where the adults were picnicking.

I was scared to death of the bully, but I waded past him into the rushing water. The bully was so surprised that he let go of the other boy. I reached down with both hands and pulled the boy up into a sitting position. He was coughing and gagging, trying to get rid of the water he'd swallowed.

As I looked around for help, I saw a man running full speed toward us, with Molcha following behind. He grabbed the boy and ran with him to the higher ground. All the picnickers had come and were watching. Molcha and I watched and waited until we were sure the boy was all right. We looked around. The bully was nowhere in sight, so we started our walk home.

I realized Babi was right—it is better to try and help someone rather than just watch, no matter how afraid I might be.

The Lekvár *Cooking*

Babi had some plum trees near her house. They were pruned low and round, no higher than a tall man. The branches reached out from a fat trunk like arms curved upward, holding their blossoms toward the sun. During the spring, the orchard looked fluffy and light, the delicate petals snow-white with a dusting of bright yellow pollen in the center. Each tree could have been a separate bouquet if you tied a bow around the trunk, but together they looked like floating white clouds. I had to sniff so hard to capture their light scent that my nostrils filled with the yellow pollen dust, but I loved to sniff it because that fragrance held a great promise. Abundant blossoms on the trees foretold a good harvest.

When the tiny petals of a blossom were carried off the trees by the light breezes of spring, they fell to the ground like delicate snowflakes. Then the fruit, smaller than a pea, soon grew to the size of a little grape. A time of watching and caring followed, because the plums attracted all kinds of insects and fungi. However, I did not get interested in the fruit until the plums had grown to their full size. Then I loved to test them. They were as hard and rubbery as wild olives. I'd bite into one, my mouth would pucker up even before the juices reached my palate, and I was never disappointed—each plum tasted as sour as sorrel. The pits were white, soft, and filled with a bitter jelly. Eating those plums was not a candy-sweet experience, but they satisfied a deep and familiar craving as nothing else could. I ate several a day, enjoying the sour taste, knowing that it would be short-lived. By July, they had turned purple on the outside and glass-green and crunchy on the inside. They were still good, but not as interesting, perhaps because I was at last permitted to eat them. I no longer had to sneak them and suffer in silence with my stomachache.

By September all of the plum trees were picked bare, as the plums were harvested into bushels, baskets, and buckets, waiting to be cooked into *lekvár*, a kind of fruit spread. The plums' heavy scent—fruity, sweet, and pungent—overpowered every other smell on the farm, enveloping not only our nostrils but our taste buds as well. Even if we ate onions, they would taste like plum nectar. All our senses were blended and held by their power.

When it was time to make the *lekvár*, Babi invited family, neighbors, and friends—Christians and Jews alike—to help her. One fall my sister Iboya, who was two years older than me, came to help us with the *lekvár*. She arrived the day we were cooking it and was added to the workforce immediately. We hardly exchanged more than smiles in passing as we scurried about helping Babi. We'll talk later, and it will be more fun, I promised myself. It will be like old times, we'll talk late into the night. Iboya and I had shared a bed at home for many years. Mother got angry with us for talking and giggling half the night. She even made us sleep head to foot, but we still managed to play toesies and giggle. I knew that Babi wouldn't mind if we talked and giggled in bed at her house. I hadn't seen Iboya all summer and Babi would understand we had a lot to catch up on.

Long makeshift tables had been set up, and the benches on both sides were crowded with women. Their hands were busy pitting the mounds of plums piled high on the tables. They were experts at this task; it was as much a part of their culture as feather plucking, cornhusking, and beating out seeds from the heads of sunflowers. The plums were squeezed between the thumb and the third finger with just the right amount of pressure to release the clean pit. The women, in high spirits and filled with excitement and anticipation, expressed their festive mood by singing the songs of the village, songs that had been passed down through generations.

The men, having dug a round fire pit and lit the firewood, gathered the pitted plums in a large copper cauldron. When it was filled, they placed it on the low burning fire. Here the age and experience of the grandfathers was

given preference over youth and strength. As they performed the activities, their sons and grandsons watched
and listened.

Babi completely ignored the cooking of the *lekvár* and
became a hostess, concerned with entertaining her guests.
She only came out of her kitchen to make sure that everyone had plenty to eat and drink. Her usually serious and
practical mood was exchanged for lighthearted gaiety. She
picked up the songs of her guests and hummed along mer-
rily in a sweet, birdlike voice as she walked to and fro. Instead of her usual dark babushka, she wore a light printed
one and let more of her cheeks show. She handed me and
Iboya trays with slices of baked pumpkin and roasted
chestnuts, and told us to distribute them among the
guests. Her face shone from all the activity as she scurried
about with steps as light as a girl's.

"How late will Babi let us stay up?" I asked Iboya.

"Oh, she'll let me stay up as long as I like," my sister
replied with great self-assurance.

"What about me?"

"Act smart, and don't ask her."

"You think she'll let me stay up as late as you?"

"Well, I'm older."

"She's in a good mood though, isn't she?"

"Everyone is in a good mood."

"They seem so . . . different," I said.

Iboya didn't comment. She was smiling at the boy to
whom she was offering her tray of sliced pumpkin. Sud-

denly she, too, looked different, almost like a grownup. Her dress was new and she had let her long blond hair hang loose around her shoulders. Watching her talk with the strange boy, I realized that she had changed over the summer. I was so busy and preoccupied with all the excitement that I hadn't noticed. She not only looked different but she talked and laughed differently. She had her head tilted back, looking up at this strange boy as she giggled at something he said. He laughed with her and steadied the tray that shook in her hands. When his hand touched hers, they both stopped laughing. I felt irritated and disgusted, bothered and confused by emotions I didn't understand.

It was now starting to grow dark and most of the other children had gone home or had fallen asleep under the long tables, deserted after the plums were all pitted. The women had rolled down their sleeves and joined the men around the glowing fire. I took my tray and offered them some treats. The women were telling stories, and the older men were taking turns stirring the *lekvár* and smoking their pipes. The *lekvár* was bubbling and splashing. Some of the women had covered their legs with rags. After the first splash hit my leg, I knew why. That splash of *lekvár* felt just like hot tar.

Night filled the fields and all the corners around the yard. The moon and stars lit up the sky, while the glow of the fire bathed everyone's face. It was a beautiful summer evening.

The young men joined the women, singing and stamping their black boots. The peasant girls swayed as they sang, clapping their hands. I was seeing more and more things not usually practiced in public. The girls were permitting the boys to put their arms around their shoulders and waists with their parents present, and no one said a thing. I seemed to be the only one not caught up in this newly developed spirit. Suddenly, I was very conscious of having been left out. I was no longer a participant, just a puzzled observer. I couldn't sort out my feelings. Why was I split off from the crowd? All my festive enthusiasm disappeared, and I felt almost abandoned.

My attention turned to the older men who were busy with the *lekvár*. It was now cooked to a consistency almost impossible to stir. A new pair of arms was needed every five minutes to stir the wooden paddle in the heavy mixture, which had grown glassy and as thick as taffy.

"It's ready, it's done!" sounded the cries in the night. "Let's lift it out and taste it, my mouth is watering." The old men gathered around the huge copper cauldron and took turns lifting up the paddle and letting the *lekvár* lazily slide back into the pot like a wide patent-leather ribbon rippling down.

"I say it could cook another couple of minutes."

"You're just looking to burn it. While you all stand around talking, it will scorch. Somebody, stir it!" The women were getting anxious.

Babi came over into the light; with her left hand she

held back her long skirt from the fire and bent over the pot. A man stopped stirring and handed her the paddle, loaded down with the heavy *lekvár*. Babi let most of it glide back, then lifted the paddle almost to eye level and examined it. She let go of her skirt, blew on the *lekvár*, and, once it was cool enough, took a large fingerful of the thick paste and stuck it in her mouth. Everyone waited in a hush. Finally, she broke the silence by announcing that it was just right.

The cauldron was immediately lifted off the fire and brought into the kitchen to cool. Babi called me to follow her inside, where she had two baskets filled with slices of her special white bread. We carried them out and set them on one of the tables, and she spooned hot *lekvár* into two bowls and stuck small wooden spatulas into them so everyone could have a taste. Babi thanked everyone for their help, then put the rest of the *lekvár* into earthenware pots to be saved for the winter.

I must have been one of the first ones to taste it; it was so hot that I winced as I swallowed. Only the layer of bread kept me from seriously burning myself. I did not realize that I was being watched until I heard loud laughter. Iboya, standing with the boy nearby, teased me, "How could you be such a baby? Couldn't you have waited until it cooled?" Some of my emotions suddenly surfaced, and it was very clear to me what I felt at that moment—resentment, anger, shame, frustration, and cowardice. Cowardice for not having the nerve to kick her.

I walked off to the side of the yard and continued to watch the others. Babi came over and put her arm around me. "I let you stay up until the *lekvár* was finished, but now it is time for you to go to bed."

"Why do I have to go to bed and not Iboya?"

"She is two years older than you."

"She was always two years older, but we went to sleep at the same time anyway."

"But now she's growing up."

"And I'm not," I said, sulking.

"I know you won't believe this, but I can appreciate the way you feel, even though I was an only child and never had a sister. God, how I used to wish for a sister ... or a brother. I was such a lonely child. But what is not meant to be just is not meant to be. That is why I wanted a houseful of children when I got married. Of course, I could not have done it without His help," said Babi, looking up toward the sky.

Then she gave me a hug and said, "I'll tell you what, two years from now you will be Iboya's age and then you can stay up as late as you want when we make the *lekvár*. Would you like that?"

"That is a long time from now."

"I know, but try to look at it this way, you still have it ahead of you. And that, all by itself, is pretty marvelous. It will be your day then, just as today is Iboya's day."

The Haircut

Babi always rose at dawn to build a fire, milk her cows, scatter corn for the chickens, and gather the eggs. While cooking us breakfast, she prompted me to recite my morning prayer, and one day when I was done she said, "Piri, it seems to me that you need to work harder to memorize the *Modeh Ani.*"

"But, Babi, it is hard to remember."

"God has more responsibilities than we do, yet we expect him to remember each of us," said Babi. She dished out our hot cereal, poured milk—still warm from the cow—from the milking bucket into an earthenware pitcher, and sat down across from me, waiting for me to look up and meet her eyes.

"I'm sorry, Babi. I promise to try harder."

"Good enough. Now, if you are willing to help me, we could bake some of the fresh corn bread that you seem to like so much before I go to join the farmers in the fields."

Remembering how delicious the bread was, even stale, I said, "I'm happy to help."

When we were done with our breakfast, Babi poured some boiling water from the iron kettle on the stove into a bowl and put in some dry cornhusks to soak so they would soften up.

"You can prepare the husks. They have to be uncoiled until they lie flat, so you can line this round pan with them. Turning them inside out will help." The husks felt silky in my fingers as I started to arrange them in the pan. "Place them so they overlap, otherwise the batter will run through," she continued. "Now use the remaining husks the same way, but lie them crosswise to be doubly sure."

As she spoke, Babi prepared the batter. She scooped freshly milled cornmeal into a bowl from a linen sack, and poured milk right from the pitcher without bothering to measure. I was amazed at how much liquid was absorbed by the cornmeal. Then she sprinkled a pinch of salt, two pinches of baking powder, and a handful of coarse sugar over the batter. She mixed it all together with her hands, then poured the batter into the pan I had prepared. Before placing it in the oven, Babi sprinkled more sugar on top.

"Don't let it get too well-done or it will crack," Babi said. "When it has a nice light golden brown color, take it out of the oven. Be sure and use the pot holders so you don't burn yourself. Let it cool at least an hour before you try to slice it, or it will crumble. There is buttermilk in the pantry. Why don't you have Molcha come over and enjoy the bread with you?"

Before I could answer, Babi was out the door, heading toward the fields.

I ran across the road to get Molcha. It was a very hot day in June. As I approached her house, I smelled the smoke of their wood-burning stove. I climbed the three mud-caked steps to the kitchen door. Molcha's mother stood by the stove, stirring something in a large pot with a wooden spoon. Her father sat at his cobbler's bench at the opposite end of the hot kitchen. Several pieces of old shoes that he'd used to cut for patches were scattered about his feet, and between his thighs he held an ankle-high shoe of maroon leather, which was stretched upside down on a cobbler's last like a cut-off foot.

He had several small wooden nails in one corner of his mouth as he returned my greeting and said, "Molcha is outside."

I found Molcha wandering about near their kohlrabi patch. Her long sun-streaked hair shone in the morning light.

"I came to ask you to come and stay with me," I said. "Babi has corn bread in the oven and I have to watch it so it won't burn. Then we can have some with a glass of buttermilk."

Holding hands, we ran across the dusty road. We could smell the sweet aroma of the corn bread as we neared the yard. I soon realized that we were not the only ones to smell the inviting aroma of the bread. Paskudniak had beat us to the kitchen. He meowed sweetly as he brushed my leg, letting me know that he was part of the family.

When the bread was golden brown, I removed it carefully with the pot holders and put it on an iron trivet to cool. As I turned around to look at Molcha, her big blue eyes were shining. She asked enthusiastically, "When can we eat it?"

"Babi said to wait an hour for it to cool," I answered.

Molcha's enthusiasm turned to disappointment. "I can't wait. It smells so good," she said.

We decided to go back to the kohlrabi patch so Molcha could show me how to eat the purple tuber. We sat down close to each other, and Molcha pulled out two kohlrabies and handed one to me. She held hers by its long leaves, bit into the tuber with her front teeth, and turned it round and round as she peeled it in one unbroken spiral. When she was finished she turned her head toward me, giving me a proud, accomplished look. We ate the fibrous tubers, but they stuck in our throats and we needed something to drink. Molcha suggested we walk to the end of their property to her grandfather's house to get a drink of water from the well.

We found her grandfather's second wife, Mrs. Peppi, shuffling about her large courtyard tossing great handfuls of corn to her large flock of cackling chickens and turkeys.

Dressed in her usual dark cotton housedress, men's shoes, and dark kerchief tied across her head, she looked cross. Reading my thoughts, Molcha shrugged as if to say, "All the same, I have to respect her."

"Good morning," Molcha called.

Mrs. Peppi, dropping the remainder of the corn from her apron, turned toward us and screamed, "You look terrible!" Molcha, startled, began to dust off the seat of her dress. "That hair—tsk, tsk, I would not be surprised if you have lice in it. Look at your friend, how neatly her hair is tied with a ribbon. A real city girl."

"Mine doesn't stay in a ribbon," Molcha protested. "It just comes undone." Mrs. Peppi wobbled her heavy body over to the porch and motioned for us to follow her.

"Sit down," she said, pushing Molcha onto a chair. Then, reaching into her sewing basket on a nearby table, she picked up a large pair of shears. Mrs. Peppi's fat fingers grabbed a fistful of Molcha's thick hair, and snipped it right below her ears in an uneven, blunt edge. She cut faster and faster so Molcha wouldn't have a chance to protest. I watched in horror as long clumps of my friend's beautiful hair fell to the ground, leaving her white neck exposed. I wondered how long it would take to blend in with her tanned face and shoulders. I didn't dare face her for fear that both of us would burst into tears.

"I'll be right back; I'm going to get a comb," said Mrs. Peppi as she shuffled into her house. She came back in a few moments with a square black comb, but its tight teeth held fast in Molcha's thick hair. Giving up, Mrs. Peppi turned away, calling over her shoulder, "Don't leave. I am going to bring you each a treat."

This reminded me of our reason for coming. "We didn't get our water," I said.

Molcha was too upset to answer. She was playing with the loose strands of hair lying on her lap.

Mrs. Peppi returned with two slices of white bread, generously spread with *lekvár*. This was a great treat—white bread on a weekday. The smooth plum spread cleared the scratchy kohlrabi fibers from our throats.

When we finished eating, we thanked Mrs. Peppi and then ran through the open fields until we were winded and threw ourselves onto the ground. We lay on our stomachs, listening to our heavy breathing and the light humming of the insects around us. Finally, Molcha broke the silence. Resting on her elbows, she swiped at the jumping grasshoppers, killing them between her palms. "I wonder if they have grandmothers?"

"I don't know."

"Anyway, they don't have hair."

Molcha wiped her palms on the grass, jumped up abruptly, and headed in the direction of her house with an exaggerated sigh. I fell into step with her, and we continued our walk in silence. When we reached her yard, she stopped and said, "I can't go in yet."

I suggested that we go to see Babi, hoping she could

fix Molcha's hair. We went to look for her in her fields. As soon as we spotted Babi talking to the wife of one of the farmers, Molcha stopped and turned to walk back. She was no more ready to face them than her own family. Babi noticed us and called for us to wait. When she reached us she looked from me to Molcha and back to me.

"What happened to Molcha's hair?" she asked.

"Mrs. Peppi cut it. Can you fix it?"

Babi took Molcha's hand as if she were a five-year-old. "Let's go back to the house. I always cut my three daughters' hair. Maybe I can even it out if my shears are sharper than your grandmother's."

"Don't you think she was mean to do this to Molcha?" I asked as we reached the yard.

"Not at all. She wanted Molcha to be cool for the summer. Look how hot it is, and Molcha has very thick, beautiful hair—not so easy to cut. Has your mother seen it?"

"No, not yet."

"You two go inside and bring a kitchen chair out to the yard, and put it in the shade of the tree."

Babi got her scissors and my large-toothed comb, tied a towel over Molcha's shoulders, and walked around her, squinting as she examined the damage. Molcha sat on the chair as still as she had when Mrs. Peppi cut her hair. Only this time she didn't look like she was going to cry. Babi snipped at the uneven ends and ran the comb over and over through Molcha's hair until she was satisfied with her work. Then she asked Molcha, "Would you like bangs? I think they would look very good with your high cheekbones."

Molcha's face broke into a shy smile as she looked up at Babi and nodded yes. With her short straight hair, and bangs over her large blue eyes, she looked just like my painted porcelain doll. I gave Babi a big hug to thank her, and ran to get Molcha my small mirror. She looked into it for a long time, turning her head slowly from side to side, and finally said, "My mother won't recognize me."

"I wouldn't worry about that," said Babi. "Mothers always recognize their children. Now, why don't you take a piece of corn bread and go wade in the Rika? You could cool off and Molcha could wash her hair."

Babi left us and went back to the fields, and Molcha and I headed to the Rika.

The Mushroom Hunt

Dawn was barely breaking when Babi gently shook my shoulder. "Come on, it's time to get going." She walked across the room to the window and stared outside. I stretched. It was cool in the little room, and I didn't feel like crawling out of my warm feather bed. But seeing Babi all dressed and ready to go, I remembered our conversation of the night before and jumped to my feet.

We had been listening to the gentle rain on the straw-thatched roof before going to bed. Babi told me that there would be plenty of mushrooms tomorrow if the rain kept up. She said that she would get the baskets ready and if I wanted to get up good and early, I could have them filled with mushrooms by the time the sun reached the barn. We could string them up and dry them so that I could take them back with me to the city. She'd told me that my mother would be happy to have them, as they could last the whole winter. I had gone to sleep full of anticipation.

I took off my warm flannel nightgown, hurried into my red gingham dress, and joined Babi by the window. "It's still so dark," I said, shivering and snuggling up to her.

"Come on," she said, "let's have some hot cereal and be on our way. There's no time to waste." She put an arm around my shoulders and led me into the kitchen.

The familiar earthenware pot was steaming on top of the stove. Babi lifted the cover and put a large wooden spoonful of the thick yellow corn mush into my bowl. Then she gave it a quick circular stir, leaving a hole in the center into which she poured milk. I was so excited that I could hardly swallow, but somehow I managed to finish all the mush in the bowl.

When I got up from the table, Babi threw a shawl over my shoulders, crossed it in front, pulled the ends under my armpits, and tied a large knot in the small of my back. She hung a basket on my arm and rushed me out into the damp morning. I began asking questions as we neared the forest. "Babi, how will I know the good mushrooms from the bad?"

"Just watch me," she said. "Try to remember the different kinds you have eaten, like *tinodi*, *galamb*, *csirke*, *keserű*. But it is also good if you just watch."

As we entered the forest, I could feel the coolness closing around us. The giant pine trees grew thick and straight up to the sky, the tops coming to points like arrows. The underbrush was thick in spots with large glossy leaves. Under my feet the dark green moss covering the tree roots felt soft and slightly damp. There were other trees scattered about with leaves of yellow, orange, and brown. Smells of growth and decay mingled in the air. Babi moved ahead of me, hunched over so that her dress brushed the ground. She was approaching a cluster of large rocks that were overgrown with ferns, climbing vines, and silvery, flat, dry moss, and soon she seemed to disappear under them. It was very still. I heard my heart thumping in my chest. I called out to Babi, "Are we there?"

"Just follow me," she called back in a reassuring tone.

I tried to walk faster, but even bent over as I was, the low branches kept scratching at my face and sticking in my hair. With my right hand dragging the basket and my left hand trying to clear a path ahead of me, I moved slowly. Finally I reached the boulders and realized that they formed the entrance to a cave. I tried to hold on to the silver moss as I eased myself in, but the moss, dry and brittle, gave way under my fingers. I was scared; I could not see Babi. I stood still, watching and listening.

"In here!" said Babi, grabbing my hand. I held on and moved inside where I could make out her silhouette by some light that filtered through the cracks between the rocks.

"See, what did I tell you? There are plenty of mushrooms in here."

I waited until my eyes got used to the darkness of the cave, and then I watched Babi's expert hands select mushrooms from the vast variety at the base of the cave walls. Some of them were half hidden under rotting leaves and roots that Babi brushed away with a quick sweep of her fingers. Then she broke off the clusters of mushrooms by gently bending them into her cupped hand.

She gave me a silent nod to go ahead. As I brushed away a rising mound of damp brown leaves that I had spotted upon entering the cave, my hands uncovered a family of orange-yellow *csirke* mushrooms. They ranged in size from about four centimeters to about eight centimeters. They looked like dwarfed whisk brooms. "Go ahead," said Babi. "Just be gentle, don't crumble them."

I put my basket down on the ground near me. Then I took the mushroom clusters one at a time, bending each one at its stem until it came away from the ground. I laid it on its side in the bottom of the basket and continued picking. Some of the *tinodi* mushrooms felt spongy and sticky. On a sudden impulse, I closed my fist over one of the smaller ones and let the wet brown meat squeeze through my fingers. Babi, looking at me, commented, "It is a sin to be wasteful."

"But it feels so smooth."

Babi shook her head from side to side, but I could see a faint smile on her face. I opened my hand to release the remains of the mushroom. "Tsk, tsk," she remarked as she gave me some leaves for wiping off my hand.

I spotted some *galamb* mushrooms, which were more conventional in shape, round caps on sausage-like stems.

They varied in color from gray to shocking pink to yellow to powder blue, and they grew individually, not in clusters, and were more uniform in size. I also found some of the plain variety called *keserü*. The hardest to find were the *tinodi* because they were brown in color and difficult to distinguish from the leaves surrounding them.

It took us close to two hours to fill our baskets heaping full. As we emerged from the shady woods, my eyes strained and blurred against the sudden light. The village, now awake, was moving toward its many tasks. Some of the villagers were walking, carrying their tools, while others were seated aboard oxen-drawn wagons, on their way to work in the fields. Their children were with them and they called greetings and asked us about the mushrooms. We waved to them and Babi answered that the mushrooms were plentiful.

When we got home, Babi got out a carving board, two knives, scissors, a large needle, and homespun thread, and put everything out on the table on the porch. I asked Babi if I could see if Molcha wanted to come over and help.

"Sure, we could use an extra pair of hands. And you can ask her to stay for lunch," Babi said.

"What are we having?"

"We'll have some *keserü* mushrooms and whatever else looks good in the garden," Babi said.

I gave Babi a big hug and kiss and ran across the road. I found Molcha under their apple tree shaking the trunk, hoping to loosen the last few apples that could not be reached without a ladder. Before I could finish explaining why I'd come, Molcha started running toward Babi's.

Molcha was excited to see all the mushrooms we had picked. Babi handed each of us one of the small knives and said, "This is not very sharp, but I still want you to concentrate on what you are doing so you don't cut yourselves."

Babi cleared the part of the table with the carving board and gave us some of the *galamb* mushrooms. She demonstrated what to do as she spoke.

"You cut off the dirty part of the stem. Then you slice them. You slice across the mushroom including the stems, and don't cut the pieces too thick or they won't dry fast enough."

Once we finished slicing the *galamb*, we scattered them on an old bedsheet to dry. Because the *csirke* mushrooms were too fragile to slice apart, Babi only had us trim the bottoms off before putting them on the sheet to dry.

Next Babi gave us the brown and spongy *tinodi* mushrooms. Molcha and I trimmed off the stems and then Babi threaded one of the needles and started to string them together, alternating each mushroom top to stem, leaving space in between for the air to circulate. Molcha and I just watched Babi because she did not trust us with this job. When she was done, Babi hung the mushrooms in the kitchen to dry.

Next she asked us to slice the *keserű* mushrooms while

she went to the garden to see what she could find to add to our lunch. When she came back, Babi sautéed the *keserŭ* mushrooms with onions, tomatoes, and bell peppers. An inviting aroma filled the house. I looked forward to lunch. When we finally ate, Molcha and I wiped up our plates with large chunks of corn bread. We both agreed it was the best meal we had ever eaten.

"Do you know why?" Babi asked.

"No, Babi, why?" I said.

"Because you have eaten the fruits of your own labor."

I wasn't sure I understood what Babi meant. But I decided not to ask any more questions. I felt satisfied inside.

The Feather Plucking

Once when I was visiting Babi in the winter, we were invited to a feather plucking at the Steins' house. It was dark outside and a gentle snow was falling as we left the house. We wrapped shawls over our heads and took a kerosene lantern to light our way. There was just enough snow on the ground to cushion our walk; the large, dry flakes drifted lazily over the scattered houses of the village. Flickers of yellow light from their small windowpanes bounced across our path, but the spaces between the houses were dark against the background of glistening snow that covered the fields. Suddenly I felt our smallness in the vast, dark space that surrounded us.

"Why are you so quiet?" asked Babi.

"It feels so lonely."

"Are you homesick?"

"No, I just feel lonely."

"This is what the country is like during the winter.

Feather plucking is one of the occasions that bring us together, and we get our comforters filled with feather down."

"Do you have feather pluckings at your house too?"

"No, *shaefele*, I haven't raised geese in many years."

"Don't you like them?"

"Geese need a big yard and they tend to be very messy. I like my yard better the way it is now. I have my vegetable garden and flowers near the house. I have the women over for an evening of sewing instead."

I pushed back my heavy shawl and let the snow brush my cheeks. Some of the large flakes settled on my eyelashes. At first they felt light and fluttery; then they grew heavy as they turned to water. Babi walked beside me, deep in her own thoughts.

We finally reached the Steins' house, which was larger and brighter than most in the village. As we neared it, I could hear voices inside. We knocked and the heavy wooden door opened halfway. Mrs. Stein poked her head out and said, "Hurry in, don't let the feathers fly." Once we were inside, she closed the door and said, "Fage, how good of you to come with your granddaughter. We'll have to give her a lesson in plucking." I smiled eagerly.

The warm room echoed with greetings from the many women, young and old, sitting around a long table covered with feathers, and a cluster of men who were seated around a stove. The women had bowls, strainers, and sieves resting in their laps. Their fingers moved so quickly, picking up and dropping feathers, that I couldn't see what they were doing with them. They made room for me on a bench and brought a chair for Babi.

"Come, Piri, watch me first," said Babi, putting an apron over her head and tying it around her narrow waist. She settled in her chair and I moved close to her. She pulled a pile of the white feathers in front of her. Sorting out the larger ones, Babi demonstrated as she spoke. "You hold it at the tip with your left hand, the thumb and middle finger. Then with the same two fingers of the right hand you grip first one side and pull down on the stem and then you do the same on the other side." Babi held a plucked quill in her left hand with just the small tip of feather left at the top.

I realized that these large plucked feathers were what made up the feather brushes that Babi used to brush beaten egg yolk on the tops of challah breads and strudels to make them golden and glossy. Each brush had about a dozen of the plucked feathers, their stems braided together, then wound with strong thread so they would not come unbraided, leaving a loop at the end to hang it with. The wing tips of the geese were also used for whisk brooms, with the small bone joint jutting out for a handle.

I tried to imitate Babi and the rest of the women, but the feather would not tear for me. "Here," suggested one of the older Stein girls, "touch your fingers to your tongue and moisten them with spit so you'll be able to grab hold of the feather." The young women were singing and the older women were reminiscing and telling stories. Even after I got the hang of it I was more interested in watching and listening than in plucking feathers. One of the men discussing crops and politics went outside and came back carrying a large pumpkin, which he dropped on the dirt floor to crack. It split in a jagged edge, revealing the thick orange meat inside. Mrs. Stein picked up a half and scooped the seeds and pulp from it into the other half. She cut the clean half into wedges and arranged them on top of the stove to bake. Then she picked up the other half and deposited it into my lap. "Here, you can pick out the seeds and put them in this strainer; then we'll wash them and roast them on a cookie sheet."

The pulp felt cool and moist as my fingers searched out the plump, slippery seeds. I loved the feel of it gliding through my fingers; it was like feeling the inside of a living thing.

One of the young women asked Babi, "Mrs. Rosner, please tell us the bride story."

Babi started to protest, but then all the women joined in, echoing, "Please, please."

"You really want to hear that story again?" she asked.

"Yes, yes, please."

Babi turned to look at me, considering whether I was old enough to hear it, and then began. "All weddings in Komjaty are exciting events, but this particular wedding was especially exciting because everyone loved the bride, Yito. She had a charitable nature in spite of being sickly, and she always found time to help the needy, never turned away a beggar, and loved children. She was truly what we call a good soul."

When Babi began the story, all hands stopped moving. The drifting feathers settled on the table in clumps. Our hostess stopped watching the sliced pumpkin on the top of the stove, the men stopped talking and moved closer to the table, and I forgot all about the pumpkin seeds.

"All the Jewish families and some of the Christian families were gathered in Yito's yard to see Yito in her bride's dress, get a look at the groom, and watch the wedding ceremony. The *chuppah*, the wedding canopy, had been set up under large shady trees to the right of the gate.

"The door of Yito's house finally opened and the groom appeared dressed in black. He was handsome—tall and straight, a yeshiva *bocher* with a farmer's build. He was not from Komjaty but came from a nearby city. He lowered his head as he walked under the waiting *chuppah* to take his place next to the bride's father and the rabbi. The door opened again and now the bride, led by her two proud grandmothers, paused for a moment on the high stoop and waved her bouquet at the excited guests. Then she stepped into the waiting crowd, and one of the grandmothers covered her delicate face with a veil. According to custom, the groom is not supposed to see the bride before the ceremony, even if he has seen her before.

"Like a cherished doll, Yito was led through the admiring crowd. Her father stepped aside to leave the groom in the center of the *chuppah* with the rabbi. The two grandmothers, each holding one of Yito's arms, walked her three times around the groom while the rabbi chanted. The grandmothers seemed to be carrying her—Yito's tiny shoes barely grazed the ground.

"Once the rabbi was finished, everyone waited in silence for the groom to finalize the marriage by breaking the glass that had been wrapped in a cloth napkin. When he brought down his foot and shattered the glass, there was a great cry of *mazel tov!*—congratulations! Then, as the crowd parted to let the couple pass through, Yito fainted and slid to the ground.

"The two grandmothers picked her up and carried her limp body inside, followed by her family and the rabbi. The door shut behind them, and the crowd outside stood confused and helpless. The groom, forgotten for the moment, had to walk up to the door and knock. It took some loud knocking before the door finally opened to let him into the house.

"The crowd waited, hoping for Yito's recovery, and the Jewish men formed a *minyan*, a quorum, and prayed. But Yito did not stir. Two men hitched up an ox wagon and began to drive to the nearest town for the doctor, knowing that they had no chance of returning to Komjaty before sundown. Tension stirred in the Jewish community: the Sabbath was drawing near, and if Yito was dead, she had to be buried before sundown, since no burial is allowed during the Sabbath."

Babi paused and looked around the hushed room before continuing. "Yito's family was in total despair. Finally the rabbi and some of the village elders declared that Yito was dead. They took her to the cemetery just as she was, dressed in her wedding clothes, and buried her. On the way back people quietly spoke among themselves. How could this have happened to a girl on her wedding day? They searched for reasons—'She should not have fasted,' 'Her dress was too tight,' or 'The sun was too hot.' But no reasoning helped to explain Yito's death, and everyone went home in a daze to finish their own preparations for the Sabbath. The groom and his family left Komjaty to return to their home.

"That night two bandits dug up the grave to steal Yito's gold wedding band. The ring would not come off her swollen finger. With a pocketknife, one of the bandits cut off her finger, and the pain was so great that Yito woke up. When she realized where she was and what had happened to her, she began to scream. The bandits ran away, leaving her alone in the blackness of the cemetery.

"Yito struggled to her feet and began walking, her gown and veil catching on shrubs and branches as she strained to see in the moonlight. Bleeding and crying, she walked until she found a break in the fence surrounding the cemetery. She tried to bandage her hand by wrapping her veil around it, but it was a very long walk to her parents' house, and she left a trail of blood along the road.

"When she reached her house, it was dark. She threw

herself on the threshold, calling, 'Let me in, let me in!' But no answer came. She banged on the door with her fist, crying, 'Mama, please let me in!' and waited in vain, mystified.

"Inside, her parents clung to each other, frozen. They thought she might be a ghost like the ones in the stories that were told in the village, or some hoodlum's prank. They could not bring themselves to open the door. When it started to get light outside they finally opened the door, only to find Yito in her tattered and bloodstained wedding dress, lying in a pool of blood. When the doctor arrived later that morning, he declared her dead. She was buried for the second time on Sunday."

Babi bowed her head. The story was over.

"Is it true that Yito used to come and haunt the house of her parents every year on the anniversary of her second burial until they both joined her in the cemetery?" asked one of the young women.

"Many people have sworn that they saw her at night walking on the road and roaming the fields near her house," someone else said. "They said that they recognized her by her torn wedding dress."

"Grandma Stein, have you ever seen her?"

"God forbid! Ptui, ptui." Grandma Stein spat to protect herself from any evil spirits that might be lurking.

Another young woman asked Babi, "Mrs. Rosner, have you seen her?"

"No, child, I haven't. I also believe that when a story is

told as often as the bride story, the storytellers tend to embellish it."

"But is the rest of it true? Was she really buried alive?"

"I wouldn't know. I am just the storyteller," Babi said, laughing.

"No more questions," Mrs. Stein said. "Let's have some pumpkin. Piri, why don't you put the pumpkin seeds on this cookie sheet?"

When it was time to go home, Babi lit the kerosene lantern and we thanked the Steins for inviting us before stepping out into the darkness of the night. It had stopped snowing. I took Babi's free hand and held on tight as we walked back home over the soft snow. I did not let go until we were inside the house.

Yahrzeit

Death first touched my life when I was only nine months old. Although I have been told that such early memories are highly improbable, I believe that I have a small but clear memory of the events that took place at that time, the time of my father's funeral. I still remember the blinders on the horses that pulled the wagon that took the whole family except me to the funeral. I also remember being nursed by our neighbor, Mrs. Parocai, who took care of me that day, and I remember my mother crying when she came to fetch me. These short but strong impressions mark my first encounter with death. After that, my growing years were laced with episodes involving death; it is one of the threads that have made up the cloth of my life.

This next story is one of my strongest and most impressionable memories of the time I spent with Babi. It still repeats in my mind whenever I question the meaning of life and death.

I was sitting in Babi's big bedroom at the end of a summer day, watching her movements and listening to her voice, calm and serene, as she went about her task. Earlier in the day she had taken her burial garments—a long white linen shirt, a gathered cap, and white stockings—out of a white box that was twice the size of a shoebox and laid them outside to air. Now she was folding them slowly on the original creases and putting them back in the box before returning it to its shelf in her wardrobe. Her face was thoughtful, as if she were remembering someone or something very sad.

"Babi, why do you keep these things?" I asked.

"We have to be ready when we are called."

"I'm not ready."

"You are a child; you have your whole life ahead of you. I am an old woman."

Just then, I realized that Babi was old. At other times, though, when I watched her sew, crochet, bake, cook, or tend the animals, I saw her as a young woman. Now I felt very sad. I did not like her looking old. "You are not old," I said out loud. "You can do things better than anybody."

Babi closed the door of the wardrobe, came over, and sat down on the bed beside me. "There is nothing sad about growing old," she said softly. "Only the privileged grow old."

"But I like you better when you are young."

"When do I seem young to you?"

"When we do things together."

"What kind of things?"

"When you teach me to crochet and tell me stories."

"I promise to crochet and tell stories later, *shaefele*, but today is Grandpa's *yahrzeit*, the anniversary of his death. Every year I prepare the *yahrzeit* lamp first before saying a prayer." Babi walked back to the wardrobe and stretched herself up on her toes, her arms over her head, her fingers searching the top shelf. Finally she gave up, pulled over a chair, and stood on its seat. I walked over and stood behind her. After probing for a few minutes at the back of the shelf, she pulled out a clear glass lamp and handed it down to me. "Be very careful, Piri, and put it on the table."

She got down from the chair, put it back in its place, and went into the kitchen. In a moment she returned with a dust cloth, a jug of kerosene, and a funnel. She put these things down on the small table beside her bed and picked up the *yahrzeit* lamp. First, she took off the hurricane glass and cleaned it. Then she pulled the old wick out of the base and threaded in a new one. Last, she filled the base of the lamp with kerosene, pouring it slowly through the funnel from the large glass jug with rope wound around it. As she reassembled the lamp, she wiped everything all over again, holding up the hurricane glass to examine it for spots.

Perhaps it was the manner in which Babi performed this task that made such a lasting impression on me. Her hands moved slowly, lingering over each step, so different from the way she usually did things. Her eyes were focused on distant thoughts, her mind far from what her hands were doing. I grew impatient, but I knew better than to interrupt, and I waited until after she had finally lit the lamp and recited a prayer in whispers. She had laid her prayer book open on a table, but she was not reading. She spoke the words from memory. Then she closed the book, put it back on the shelf, and sat watching the yellow flame for a while, her small brown hands lying idle in her lap. With a sigh, she said very quietly, "Well, it is all done."

"Can we talk now, Babi?"

"All right, Piri," she said. "Go, bring me the crochet basket."

I got it and handed her the fine hook with the delicate piece of lace she was working on, and took out my own thick hook and the length of chain I was struggling with.

"Babi, will Grandpa really come here during the night?" I asked, hoping desperately that Babi would say, "No, of course not—it's just a custom." I had seen *yahrzeit* lamps lit before, but I never had to sleep in the same room with one. I was scared, but some part of me secretly wanted to be a witness this time, to watch from an undetected corner as the small white bird came in the dead of night to pay a call on his family.

"What a question!" said Babi, shaking her head in disbelief.

"Well, will he?"

"Who told you such a thing?"

"Iboya."

"What did she tell you?"

"Well, I remember when Mother lit the *yahrzeit* lamp for Grandpa last year . . ."

"Go on."

"I remember the whole house was dark except for the small flame from the lamp. Everyone was asleep. Iboya and I crept out of our bed and brought our pillows and covers to the doorway of the living room where the lamp was lit. We decided to stay up and wait for Grandpa's soul to come in the form of a white bird. That is when Iboya told me."

Babi shook her head again. "What did she tell you?"

"That every person has a soul and that the soul is what keeps us alive. When we die, the soul flies out of us and leaves the body. I asked Iboya how the soul got out and she told me that it flies out through the mouth. That's why people die with their mouths open."

Babi had stopped her crocheting and was just listening.

"Iboya said that if the person has been good and has led a pious life, the soul goes to heaven immediately and becomes an angel. But if he has been bad and has committed sins, his soul goes to hell."

"It's not that simple," said Babi, still shaking her head from side to side. "Only Moses went straight to heaven. The rest of us have sins, I'm afraid."

"Iboya said the soul becomes a bird like a small white dove, and it is allowed to go home for a short visit once a year on the eve of the anniversary of its death. Is it true, Babi?"

"As usual, you've got some truth and a lot of nonsense."

"What part is true?"

"That the soul leaves the body after death."

"Does it come back to visit?"

"I don't know anything about that."

"Does the soul go up to heaven after it leaves the body?"

"Not right away. We have to pray for it. That is why we say Kaddish, the prayer for the dead, for eleven months after a person dies. After that the soul gets God's forgiveness. We also say Kaddish each year on the anniversary of a person's death. This way we remember them."

"Does the soul look like a small bird?"

"We don't know what the soul looks like."

"But is it a bird?"

"We don't know."

"Then why do people say it is?"

"Piri, people say lots of things. I suppose they guess that it must be a bird because it rises to God's throne."

"Why do we light the *yahrzeit* lamp?"

"The *yahrzeit* is a reminder of the anniversary of death. The light is a reminder of the light of the soul."

"Is the soul a light?"

"There are many things written in books that say that the soul is a light, and that man is guided by this light.

Every night the soul travels out of our body while we are asleep, but leaves just enough light inside us to keep us alive."

"Where does the soul go?"

Babi put down her crocheting, went to the shelf that held her prayer books, took one down, and turned the pages until she found what she was looking for. "It goes up to God and reports our daily deeds, which are written in the big book that stands beside his throne."

I was horrified.

"Here is the prayer for Yom Kippur, the Day of Atonement," Babi said. "It says that God wrote in the book and everyone signed it."

"Wrote what?"

"Your deeds. The good deeds, as well as the sins."

I was shocked. I had a vision of a firebird sneaking out of my helpless sleeping body and flying up to God. God sat on a great gold chair, wearing gold-and-purple garments and an elaborate crown that was studded with jewels of every possible color. He was big, and in spite of his long white beard, his features were ruddy and robust. He was ancient, but not old; he did not have wrinkles or other signs of old age. His flowing beard and his great head of white hair gave him an air of authority, and he radiated self-assurance and power. There were many angels around him whose childlike faces were not quite young; they looked like the ones I had seen on the stained-glass windows of the churches and synagogues in our city. The angels played their harps, but God was not listening to them. He was leafing through a huge black book resting in his lap. Its gold-edged pages contained a long list. At short intervals, different birds appeared, encased in sheaths of flame. These birds had no feathers; they were just dark shadows inside crimson flames. God would nod in greeting and pause at a page. The wing of each shadow reached for the large gold pen extended to it by a servant's hand, took the pen, and signed on a half-filled page. When the bird finished writing, God nodded again, the wing returned the pen to the extended hand, and the firebird flew downward.

"Is that how God keeps track of us, in a book?" I had always wondered how he could know everything we did. "I don't like souls."

"A minute ago you did not know what a soul was, and now you tell me that you don't like them. What don't you like?"

"They are sneaky."

"Souls are sneaky."

"Yes. They tell on their own person."

Babi chuckled. "How could you accuse souls of being sneaky? That is their mission. It is all God's will."

"Just the same, I don't like them."

"I tell you what, Piri. I'll make you a promise that when you grow up and learn more, you'll change your mind."

I have been a grownup now for a long time, and I have learned many things. Death has continued to weave its thread into the fabric of my life, but my understanding of the soul has not broadened and my questions remain unanswered. Maybe I still haven't grown up enough.

For Babi my greatest hope is that her unquestioning trust in God sustained her through her own terrible last hour, when she was taken away from the home and land she loved so much by the Nazis. And I pray that she forgives me for not sharing her strong faith. Wherever she is, and wherever I go, I hope she knows how I remember her in my heart.

RECIPES

Here are some recipes inspired by these stories. You will need to have a grownup help you with them, just like Babi used to help me.

CHALLAH

I used to love to watch Babi make the challah on Fridays. Her small brown hands would fly like a magician's. As she folded the braids together, I would beg her to slow down so I could follow how she did the six-strand braiding, but she said, "I can't because if I slow down, I get all mixed up and have to start all over again. But don't worry, I'll teach you in good time before you get married." Babi never did give me her recipe, so here is a recipe I have used, from my cousin Ilene Slapen. It just has a three-strand braid.

Ingredients
¼ C. sugar
2¾ tsp. dry yeast
¾ C. warm water
3 tsp. vegetable oil
2 eggs at room temperature
1 tsp. vanilla
3 C. unbleached or bread flour
1½ tsp. salt
cornmeal

Dissolve the sugar and yeast in the warm water in a large bowl, and let stand 10 minutes until foamy. Beat the oil, eggs, and vanilla together. Put two tablespoons of the egg mixture aside, and add the rest to the yeast mixture, stirring with a whisk. Add the flour and salt and stir until smooth.

Turn the dough out onto a lightly floured surface. Knead it for about 10 minutes, until smooth and elastic. Place the dough in a large greased bowl. Cover with a dish towel and let rise in a warm, draft-free place for about one hour, or until the dough doubles in size. To check if the dough has risen enough, press two fingers into it. If the indentation remains, the dough is ready for the next step.

Punch the dough down and shape it into a ball. Return the dough to the bowl. Cover and let rise for one hour or until doubled in size.

Punch the dough down again and turn it out onto a lightly floured surface. Divide the dough into three equal balls, cover, and let them rest for 15 minutes.

Roll out each ball into a 12-inch rope, tapered at each end and slightly fat in the middle. As you finish rolling out the rope, roll it through some flour. Pinch the top ends of the ropes together, and braid the pieces just like you would braid hair. When you reach the end of the dough, join the ends of the ropes and pinch them together.

Place the challah on a baking pan lightly covered with cornmeal to prevent sticking. Cover it and allow it to rise until it has doubled in size.

Position rack in the center of oven and preheat to 375 degrees. Brush the raised challah with the reserved eggs. Using a spray bottle, mist the oven with water two times and place the challah on the rack. Let bake for 10 minutes. Then reduce the heat to 350 degrees and continue to bake for 15 to 20 minutes. Every oven is different, and baking times vary. The challah is done when a wooden toothpick inserted in the center comes out clean.

LÁNGOS

On the days when she baked new bread, Babi would make lángos *for breakfast. It was made from a piece of the bread dough and baked in the brick oven. These days, because people no longer have brick ovens,* lángos *is usually fried in oil, like in this recipe. Use a bit of challah dough or, if you are baking another kind of bread, use a bit of that dough to make* lángos.

Ingredients
Bread dough
Oil for deep frying

Allow the dough to rise. Punch it down and then take a piece about the size of a fist and pat it until it is a round disk about one inch thick. Heat oil in a pan, then drop the dough into the hot oil and cook until golden brown on both sides.

ARANKA'S CHICKEN SOUP

When I make chicken soup, I remember Babi working in her kitchen, excited about welcoming the coming Sabbath. I like to add a touch of dill to my soup to make its aroma close to the wonderful aroma of Babi's soup. Even in the winter, when fresh vegetables were not available, she would always have some dried dill to add to whatever else she had managed to preserve from her garden during the summer.

Ingredients
1 large onion
4 carrots
4 celery stalks
3 parsnips
5 sprigs broad-leaf parsley
1 sprig of fresh dill
1 3-pound chicken, cut into eight pieces. Free-range
   or kosher chicken recommended
1 T. kosher salt
1 tsp. white pepper
1 T. saffron (optional)
water
1 box fine-cut egg noodles

Peel the onion and cut it into four quarters. Scrub the carrots well and cut diagonally into 2-inch pieces. Peel the celery with a vegetable peeler to remove the strings and cut diagonally into 2-inch pieces. Peel the parsnips and cut diagonally into 2-inch pieces. Tie stems of the parsley and dill together with kitchen string or white thread.

Remove and discard the skin and excess fat from the chicken. Wash chicken well in cold water. Put it in a 6- or 8-quart pot. Add water to cover chicken. Set the pot on the stove and cover. Bring it to a boil on medium heat, then skim off the foam that comes to the top. Repeat if necessary to have a nice, clear broth. Add all other ingredients except the noodles to the pot. Then add water to cover the vegetables and put cover on the pot. Lower heat and simmer the soup for approximately one and a half hours. To tell if the soup is done, check one of the thighs to see if the joint is clean and the meat comes easily off the bone.

At this point, take the chicken out of the soup. You can cut it up and put the pieces into the soup, or make chicken salad or have it with cranberries or applesauce.

Cook the egg noodles according to the directions on the box, and add a heaping serving spoonful to each bowl of soup just as you serve.

CORN BREAD

Babi made her corn bread without measuring—she knew by looking and feeling exactly how much of each ingredient she needed. Here is a recipe for those of us who need a little more guidance.

Ingredients
1½ C. cornmeal
2½ C. milk
2 C. all-purpose flour
1 T. baking powder
1 tsp. salt
⅔ C. brown sugar, plus 1 T. for topping
2 eggs
½ C. vegetable oil

Preheat oven to 400 degrees. Combine cornmeal and milk in a small bowl and let stand for 5 minutes. Grease a 9 × 13 inch baking pan.

In a large bowl, combine flour, baking powder, salt, and sugar. Stir the cornmeal mixture into the dry ingredients, then add the eggs and oil and stir until smooth. Pour batter into the pan. Sprinkle 1 tablespoon of brown sugar on top.

Bake corn bread for 30 to 35 minutes, or until a knife inserted into the center of the corn bread comes out clean.

LECSÓ WITH MUSHROOMS

Lecsó is one of the most popular Hungarian dishes. When Babi made it, her ingredients varied based on the seasons. Here is one of my favorite combinations.

Ingredients

2 green bell peppers
1 red bell pepper
1 yellow or orange bell pepper
10 oz. small portobello mushrooms
1 large onion
3 or 4 plum tomatoes
⅓ C. vegetable oil
1 or 2 garlic cloves (peeled and crushed)
1 T. kosher salt
½ tsp. fresh ground pepper
1 T. sweet paprika

Prepare the peppers by washing them, cutting them in half, and removing stem, seeds, and pulp. Cut them into ½-inch slices. Don't wash the mushrooms; instead, wipe them with a slightly damp paper towel. Cut the mushrooms in half. Peel the onion, cut it in half, then cut it into ½-inch slices. Cut the tomatoes in half. Heat half of the oil in a deep frying pan or wok and sauté peppers, onions, and garlic approximately 10 to 12 minutes. Put the sautéed vegetables in a large bowl. Add the remainder

of the oil to the pan, reheat, and sauté mushrooms approximately five minutes. Add tomatoes and sauté approximately five minutes. Return peppers, onions, and garlic to
the pan. Sprinkle with salt, pepper, and paprika, and cook
for approximately five more minutes. Serve over boiled
wide noodles, rice, or barley. *Lecsó* is also good on baked
potatoes or as a side dish with meat or fish.

ROASTED PUMPKIN SEEDS

Roasted pumpkin seeds are a wonderful treat in the fall and winter. Make some for your friends, as Mrs. Stein did when she had friends over to help with feather plucking.

Ingredients
Pumpkin seeds
Vegetable oil
Salt (optional)

Preheat oven to 300 degrees. Scoop the seeds out of the pumpkin, rinse them, and spread them on a paper towel to dry. Cover a cookie sheet with aluminum foil and spread the seeds over the foil. Spray the seeds lightly with vegetable oil and sprinkle with salt. Bake until you hear the first seed pop, then stir the seeds and bake for a few minutes more, until lightly toasted. Total baking time is about 10 to 12 minutes. Let the seeds cool before you taste them!